THE IRON MARSHALL

Farmington hadn't seen a shooting in six years. Then Dan McQuade hit town. Sixty minutes later there was a badge on his shirt, violence in the streets and blood on his hands. Farmington erupted into a blaze of gunfights, and it took an iron marshall to keep the town from being shot right off the map.

THE IRON MARSHALL

Steven C. Lawrence

GUNSMOKE

This hardback edition 2008
by BBC Audiobooks Ltd
by arrangement with
Golden West Literary Agency

ISBN 978 1 405 68249 7

British Library Cataloguing in Publication Data available.

Printed and bound in Great Britain by
CPI Antony Rowe, Chippenham, Wiltshire

1

THE LAST OF THE DAY was a wide band of golden light when McQuade drew up in the cover of the willows lining the Platte. Below him, the river, a hundred yards wide and a foot deep, gurgled sluggishly over the grayish tongues of sand bar. Behind, the Nebraska prairie stretched long and flat to the western horizon, quiet and peaceful ilke the town ahead. McQuade wondered how long it would stay that way once he rode in.

The brief thought was gone as he turned his buckskin down the bank. By crossing this way, he could enter along Farmington's rear side and avoid immediate notice. He knew the town, made and kept alive by the Union Pacific. It had always been quiet, had never suffered the wildness and growing pains of other railheads like Ogallala and Ellsworth and Dodge, had never known the trouble a gun like his own could bring to a town.

He thought again of the chances he had of not bringing that trouble. Only a few days and he'd know, and maybe in a year or two nobody would remember where he'd gone. He'd pictured himself, often enough in his long ride, behind a breaking plow, gee-hawing a pair of mules, going back to a home each night instead of four bare walls of a hotel room. . . .

On the east bank McQuade kept to the cottonwoods and willows, accepting the clouds of mosquitoes that deluged him as part of the price of riding in unnoticed. He was a long man, close to forty, with leathery skin that showed years of living outside in the weather. He wore a dusty blue serge suit, the trousers tucked into high black boots. The wide brim of his Stetson curled down in front and half hid his serious face. His eyes, gray and set deep, were as habitually cautious as the hand he rested an inch from the stock of the Winchester booted beneath his right knee.

The town noises came to him as he circled around the long line of flat, false-fronted buildings to Union Street. Once in the business district, his attention was drawn to the posters tacked onto doors and fences and walls, all advertising Major Clint Carson's Wild West Show. He was looking at the inked pictures of Indians and cavalry and cowboys when the first loud clang of iron startled him.

Instinctively, his right hand dropped the rein and began to fall back. Then, catching himself, he swung the buckskin toward the livery.

The blacksmith, a thick-chested man wearing a leather apron over his pants, looked up from the twisted wagon iron he'd been pounding into shape. He wiped one hairy arm across the sweat that beaded his forehead.

McQuade asked, "Can you handle my horse?"

The man's eyes went over him, inventorying him item by item. He motioned at the buckskin. "Them shoes should be checked, too. That'll be extra."

"Of course. Whatever you think he'll need." McQuade swung down from the saddle. His hunched shoulders relaxed a bit now that his back was to the high, windowless barn.

"My hostler'll handle him," the blacksmith said. He called into the double row of stalls. "Seth. Hey, Seth."

McQuade bent and pulled the trousers from his boots. He brushed the trail dust from each leg, looked toward the pump and through beyond the door. "I'd appreciate the use of the pump to get this dirt off."

"Use all you want." The blacksmith glanced at the short, thin man who'd come out of the barn, a man who had an unusually long face, clean-shaven and very square. "Seth, give this water and a rub. Use the back stall."

Seth Perrault raised one hand to the reins, but the hand stopped halfway up. His eyes were fixed on McQuade. "You're Marshal McQuade," he said. "You are. I saw you two, three years ago when you visited Ben Ford."

"That's right," McQuade answered quietly.

"But you aren't due for two days. We were told Sat'day."

"I thought if I got in early, I could get used to the town by Saturday."

The long face frowned. "Well, we weren't sure you'd come. Bein' hunted like you are. We didn't think—"

"Take it inside, Seth," the blacksmith said. "Go ahead."

6

"I don't see why," the hostler argued. "They got a barn behind the jail. He should keep his horse there."

"Take him," the blacksmith insisted. "Now, Seth."

For a few moments silence lay hard between them. Finally, the hostler gripped the reins and led the buckskin into the barn.

Without a word the blacksmith turned back to the wagon iron on the anvil. McQuade walked to the pump, took off his hat and coat and brushed the dust from them before hanging them over the handle. He rolled up his sleeves, dropped his hands into the trough and splashed water over his face. He shook his fingers dry and used his handkerchief to wipe the last wetness from his forehead. When he went to pick up his coat, he heard the blacksmith's voice.

"There's a no-gun law in this town, Mr. McQuade."

McQuade looked around. The blacksmith pointed to the .44 Colt holstered on McQuade's right hip, tied to his thigh.

"You saw how some people here feel," the blacksmith added. "Might be best if you shucked that 'til you start wearin' a badge."

"You figure there's no chance of getting a permit?"

"Might be. Billy Ford's actin' marshal 'til you take over." His wide face shifted to the deep shadows of the barn. "Better see 'bout that rifle, too. That law covers all guns."

McQuade nodded. He put on the Stetson and coat. Then he unbuckled his gunbelt and draped it over his right shoulder, making certain the holster hung down across his chest so the Colt would still be ready for a draw.

The blacksmith said, "They might be filled up at the hotel." He gestured at the three windows above the doorway. "I got some rooms the farmers use when they stay overnight."

McQuade smiled slightly, but there was no mirth in it. "Obliged," he said. He turned and went into the barn.

His buckskin was in the last stall, its saddle and bridle still on. McQuade walked back along the double rows of stalls, made certain the hostler wasn't attending to something else. He passed the buckskin and opened the rear door, then edged around the doorjamb into the daylight. There was no sign of movement. Every door at the back of the adjoining building was closed.

McQuade returned to the buckskin. The hostler hadn't even started on the cinch before he'd left. There had been a time in Dan McQuade's life when he would have gone after the hostler and asked some questions. Now he dismissed the thought, because the last thing he wanted to show in Farmington was belligerence. He drew the Winchester from its boot and rested it against the stall. Then he began taking the saddle off his horse.

Seth Perrault moved hurriedly through the crowded bar of the Granger Hotel to the front table where two men sat playing cribbage. The player close to the window, dressed in Eastern-made clothes, was a harness and bridle drummer who'd come in that morning. The other was Tom Gruber. He was about Seth's age, but he was as heavily built as the hostler was thin. Gruber had a thick black mustache, which hid the movements of his mouth as he invited Seth to sit down.

Seth didn't sit. He muttered quick words to Gruber.

Gruber glanced carefully at the drummer. "You sure he's McQuade?"

"Course I'm sure. Dammit, I say somethin's gotta be done 'bout him. He's got no right comin' here with gunmen huntin' him."

"Gunmen?" the drummer repeated. His dark, tight-skinned face shifted from Seth to Gruber. "What's this about gunmen?"

"It's our new marshal," Gruber told him. "Name's McQuade." You might'ye read about him. He killed two of the Clinton brothers in a Tombstone robbery three months ago."

"That ain't all," Seth added. "Jake Clinton bushwacked McQuade a couple weeks after. Shot him up so bad they had to keep him in the gov'ment hospital at Yuma so's Clinton couldn't finish the job. The day McQuade left the hospital he got shot at. I say with gunmen chasin' him, he's got no right comin' here."

"All right. All right, Seth," said Gruber, standing to look out the window. Beyond the hotel the building's shadow stretched long and wide to the opposite board-walk. The last rays of the setting sun reflected in a fiery orange and reddish glare from the windows above the livery doorway. The same sun made the front stalls clearly visible, but Gruber couldn't see anyone except the black-smith.

"He hasn't come out yet?" Gruber said to Seth.

"He's bein' plenty careful. He knows he's bein' hunted. I say you oughta do somethin'."

"There's nothin' I can do."

"You been talkin' enough against McQuade. I figured . . ."

"I got nothin' to do with the law now. Remember?" Gruber's eyes flicked to the drummer, still seated at the table. When he looked at Seth again, a frown lined his mustached face. "You better wait till McQuade comes out. After, go tell Mayor Appell."

Gruber didn't wait for an answer. He pushed his way through the batwings and started crossing Union toward the two-story wooden building that had *Weekly Tribune* painted in high black letters along the false front. He'd reached the newspaper porch before he realized that the drummer had followed him outside and across the street.

Gruber hesitated, waited for the other man to catch up. "Look," he said. "You know what English said."

"What, that hostler? He thinks I'm followin' just to see what you're gonna do." He moved ahead of Gruber now, onto the porch and into the building.

The *Tribune* office was one huge room with a desk and table heaped high with newspapers in front, several type cases along the right wall and a large two-page press in back. A tall man wearing dust cuffs on the sleeves of his white shirt was bent over a type case. He glanced around as the door opened. He was about forty, his face tanned and handsome with fine, even features. His warm eyes cooled when he saw who'd come inside.

"What are you two trying to do?" he asked in a low voice.

"McQuade's in town, Mr. English," Gruber answered, then quickly repeated what Seth Perrault told them. "I figured you'd want to—"

"We'll have to change things," the drummer interrupted. "There's no chance of me duckin' McQuade for two days. Not in a town this small."

"Voci, that's still no reason for all of us to be seen together like this," said English tightly. "The last place we should all be is in this office."

Calem Voci muttered a curse, his eyes suddenly nar-

9

rowed and unfriendly. "Don't worry. You won't be connected to it. I'll get Red and Jessup, and we'll kill him before he leaves that barn."

English, who normally showed no emotion, had a slight frown on his face. "No. Not in the livery. This can't look like a setup. It's got to look right. With witnesses."

"Witnesses, hell. There ain't time for witnesses."

"No. That's final," English said. "Don't you forget I was the one who went to Jake Clinton. I got McQuade to come here, and we'll do it my way."

"Hey, there he goes," Gruber broke in. The others followed his finger, pointed out into the street. McQuade had left the livery and was crossing Union toward the jail. The holstered six-gun was draped over his shoulder, and he held his right hand up close to his stomach, inches from the Colt's butt.

"He'll be inside awhile," said Gruber. "Probably'll go back to the house to see Ben Ford's daughter." His voice dropped off. He looked worriedly at English, as though he'd said something wrong.

Their stares locked. The veins in English's neck tightened, but he said nothing to Gruber.

"How 'bout a back way to the house?" Voci asked Gruber.

"Yes. By the barn from Depot Street."

"Then, that's it," Voci said. "Me and Jessup go in through the office. Red'll use the barn. And we get him right in the middle."

"No," English told him quickly. "That way there'd be questions. It could scare Stillwell."

Voci uttered another curse. "Listen, Jake set this up mainly to get McQuade. The bank comes after that."

"Not with me, it doesn't," English snapped. "You remember that."

Silence fell, then stretched out as English walked to the front window. He stood without moving for almost a minute, his eyes on McQuade. Finally he turned and said to Gruber, "Billy Ford should be making a round now. What time will he be at the hotel?"

"Five, ten minutes. After he checks upper Union."

English nodded, turned to face Voci. "You make trouble Billy can't handle, McQuade'll have to step in. You'll have time to get your guns and get set up in the hotel saloon."

"Saloon, hell," Voci spat. "He'd never expect anyone to come at him through a jail office. He'd be watchin' too close in a saloon."

"There'll be three of you," English said, and he smiled. "No man can watch that well. Not even McQuade."

In the doorway of the marshal's office, McQuade took one last glance behind him. He saw no sign of the hostler. The Farmington men and women he'd passed had shown no special interest in him, so he figured no harmful word had spread ahead of him.

McQuade let himself relax. Actually, it didn't bother the people to see a stranger in their town. Because the newspapers had made so much of the Clinton trouble, it was natural for a few like the hostler to talk against his becoming marshal. All he needed was time, a few quiet days without any trouble. He'd just have to be careful to make sure things went that way.

Once McQuade saw the office was empty, he continued on through. When he opened the rear door to the yard, he felt a thin, nervous tick in his throat.

Near the porch of the house back there, a small boy was throwing a stick for a mongrel puppy to chase. Suddenly, attracted by McQuade's footfall, he turned and stared at the gunbelt and holster draped across McQuade's chest.

"Mommy," the boy called into the house. "Mommy."

McQuade halted. The six-year-old, a hatless towhead in checkered shirt and blue jeans, stepped back to the porch. He didn't touch the stick the puppy dropped at his feet.

"I used to have a dog myself," McQuade said. He took off his hat, bent and picked up the stick. "Down in Texas, when I was about your age." He threw the stick in a careful arc toward the open barn doorway.

The boy watched the yelping pup chase after it. His narrowed blue eyes lost their worry.

"You made it sail just like a kite," he said.

"Sure." McQuade smiled. "That gives the dog a chance to start off before it hits the ground."

The boy laughed happily. "I'll do it that way." Behind him the screen door opened, and a young woman with ash-blonde hair appeared. She held one hand up to her face, shading her eyes against the sun.

McQuade's heart gave a thump, his mind filled with

11

hopeful anticipation, with something more. A look of surprise came over the woman's pretty face, but the expression betrayed no emotion. She started down the stairs.

McQuade said, "Hello, Ann."

"Hello, Dan." She stopped beside the boy and put one hand on his shoulder. She smiled, but the smile was strained, and concern was clear in her eyes. "Stevie, this is Mr. McQuade. He knew Mommy a long time ago."

The boy's eyes widened. "You're Marshal McQuade. You're goin' to take my Uncle Billy's place."

"That's right, Stevie."

"My grandpa was marsh'l here. My daddy was a lawman, too."

McQuade nodded. "I knew Steve Heath, boy. Your father was a good lawman."

Stevie looked at his mother. "He knew Dad before he died, Mommy."

"I know," Ann Heath said, her face calm and restrained. "Supper is on the table. Wash your hands and get ready."

"But, Mommy—"

"Go ahead, Steven."

Reluctantly, the boy turned and started up the steps, his little puppy tagging along behind him. When he reached the porch, he turned again. "I'll see you, Marsh'l."

"I'll see you, Steve."

Ann Heath waited until the screen door closed behind her son before her level hazel eyes returned to McQuade. "We didn't expect you until Saturday."

Nodding, he looked at the boxes, tied with lengths of lariat, piled in the corner of the porch. "You're moving out."

"The town owns this house. Whoever is marshal lives here. Billy will only be your deputy."

"I wasn't thinking about your brother. You know how I feel. That hasn't changed."

She stood quietly. For a second her eyes stayed on the flat planes of his dark-burned face and his black hair parted deep on the side. Then they shifted to the gunbelt and Colt. "We've heard a lot of talk about the Clintons. You didn't come in early to see if they could be waiting?"

"Is that all you believe there is to it?"

12

"I know how you have to live. What am I supposed to believe?"

"I wanted to live here before I took over," he answered softly. "I figured once the people accepted me, talk couldn't hurt." His gaze moved to the marshal's office and back to her. "I was going to ask you to stay."

Ann was silent. Her eyes looked away, closed. "We went all through that, Dan. I had enough while I was married to one lawman."

"It's been six years. Times have changed. And this is a quiet town. It would be better, easier."

"For how long? Until the Clintons come? Or until you're forced to go after someone with your gun?"

"We could try, Ann."

"Try?" She sighed, odd hard lines suddenly shading the beauty of her face. She was very close to him, and she pulled away, held herself rigidly. "I've thought of you. You were so good to us those last few months."

"I looked for you. I came to see your father twice. I kept in touch with him, but he never sent a word."

"I asked him not to." She stared up at him and shook her head slowly. "I taught school in Omaha. If you had come and said you were through with the law, I might have—I don't know," she whispered. "I came back when my father got sick. I've found—Stevie's known only quiet people, not men who need a gun strapped around their waist to keep alive."

She stopped talking, and he said, "There's another man?"

Ann nodded. "George English, who owns the newspaper, has asked me to marry him. He's a good man. He'd even go to Omaha if I want."

McQuade straightened stiffly. "Ann, I only mean to hold this job until I'm positive things—" His words broke off, his eyes becoming frozen on the jail doorway. The figure of a man had entered the office from the street, the bulk of his body silhouetted against the sunlight for only an instant, making it impossible for McQuade to recognize him.

A second, shorter man followed the first inside. McQuade edged to the left, placing his body between Ann and the office. He'd evaluated the pair, one tall and bulky, the other short, always trailing behind. His right hand

13

rose, pulled the gunbelt lower, then remained inches from the Colt's butt.

The bulky figure filling the doorway was Mayor Appell, a fat, graying man whose flushed face was pinched with concern. His companion was Seth Perrault. When Appell saw McQuade his round face broke into a wide grin.

"I was told you were here, Marshal," he said loudly. "I've got your badge right in here. Come in. Come in."

McQuade's body relaxed, his hand dropping to his side. He turned to face Ann, but the spot where she'd stood was empty. She'd already gone onto the porch.

"Ann," McQuade said. "Ann?"

Ann opened the screen door, stepped inside and let it close behind her.

2

MAYOR APPELL MOVED BACK FROM the doorway to let McQuade come into the office. "We expected you'd be on the train that's bringing Carson's show, Marshal."

"I always look a town over before I start my job," McQuade said, shaking the mayor's outstretched hand. "It's better for the town, safer all the way around."

Seth Perrault watched, the hostility still on his face. "What 'bout gunmen, Appell? They ain't best for this town."

"Oh, forget it, Seth," Appell told the hostler. "You let me handle this."

"We already let you handle enough, dammit. You know what I think."

"Oh, go ahead, Seth. Go ahead. You keep your nose out of official business."

The mayor stood in silence while Seth stepped onto the boardwalk. Then Appell went to the rolltop desk and began fingering through the cubbyholes. When he looked at McQuade again, he was holding out the tarnished marshal's badge he'd taken from the desk.

"Just raise your right hand," he said.

McQuade shook his head. "Not till June first, Mayor. Young Ford can handle things three more days."

"It would be better if you took over. Billy isn't doing the job his father did."

"He's been handling it two months. Town seems quiet enough."

Through the office window he could see that the lamps burning on the opposite porches were already lightening the first gray of nightfall. Seth Perrault had stopped to talk to four men who'd been passing the hotel. Three of them stared toward the jail with deep interest. The fourth had already crossed Union to Farmington's second saloon, bursting with the information that Dan McQuade was in town.

Silently, McQuade cursed the hostler for the way he was building things up. He looked at Appell and laid one hand against the gunbelt. "All I want is a permit to wear this."

Appell sighed and put the badge on the desk. "You won't need a gun until you take over. Not here."

"Mayor. You knew about the Clintons when you hired me. I'd be a fool to go around unarmed."

Appell's eyes tightened a little. "Well, if you think—" He paused and went on in a strained voice, "Billy'll be around the hotel. We'll get the permit over there."

The hotel lobby was small and clean, with a leather-covered couch and four leather chairs placed about it. The door on the right led to the saloon, and a few feet beyond was a staircase rising to the second floor. A chandelier threw its dim light across two ancient lithographs on the left wall. The registration desk held only a leather-bound ledger, which the clerk reversed for McQuade to sign.

"Only rooms left are upstairs," the clerk said pleasantly. "We're almost filled up, with Major Carson takin' so many rooms. And all the drummers who're in for the show."

"I'd like one downstairs in back as soon as I can," said McQuade. "One with a window."

The clerk closed the ledger and smiled. He was a little man of seventy whose flat nose was built into a face streaked with small reddish veins. At the outbreak of laughter from the saloon, he glanced that way.

"If you play poker, Mr. McQuade, you c'n always find a friendly game goin' on."

Appell touched McQuade's arm. "Billy Ford's in there."

McQuade had heard the cursing mixed with the laughter. Stepping to the saloon doorway, he could see the glint of the star on the chest of the heavy-set man who stood talking to three card players at a wall table. One was a drummer, from his clothes, the others cowhands dressed in Levis and faded dark shirts. All their faces were shadowed in the thick tobacco smoke, but McQuade knew they were giving the deputy some back talk.

The group of drinkers lined opposite the back-bar mirror shifted their attention from the table to McQuade.

16

Seth Perrault, standing in the middle, left the others and walked hurriedly toward the lobby.

He waved one hand at the card players. "See what I mean, Appell? McQuade's here a half hour and there's trouble already. Them cowhands are both packin' guns."

"They're strangers, Seth. So's the drummer. They might not know about the no-gun law."

"They know all right. The barkeep told them. So did Billy." He paused at the louder, vile language one of the cowhands was using and stared hard into McQuade's eyes. "Well, Marsh'l, you gonna let them run all over that kid?"

"Hold it, Seth," Appell said. "McQuade isn't—"

"He ain't bein' paid t' jest stand here," Seth snapped. His angry challenging stare shifted to the table, then returned to McQuade. "We're paying high for that gun reputation of yours, McQuade."

The corners of McQuade's mouth tightened. He passed the gunbelt to Appell.

"Hold this," he said. And he started into the saloon.

The men at the bar were quiet, so still McQuade could hear their breathing. The sound was heavy and labored. They'd waited for him to come in, he realized. They'd expected he'd have to help young Ford. He knew their type. They'd group in around him, try to put him on the spot, their hungry eyes weighing and judging him, asking, "How'll you handle this? Are you as good as they say you are?"

He heard the deputy say, "Come on now, take them off."

The well-dressed man sitting with his back to McQuade said, "Let me handle this. These cowboys won't cause any trouble."

Billy Ford asked again, "Come on. I'll check them for you."

"Oh, get the hell on your way," the shorter, red-headed cowhand snarled. He swore obscenely and added, "You'll git a busted head 'fore I give up my guns."

"Hold it right there," McQuade said loudly. "There's an ordinance against carrying a gun in this town, cowboy."

"Who the hell's this?" the redhead began.

"Take them off," McQuade ordered. "Like the law says."

17

His eyes flicked to the well-dressed man and the second cowhand. Both had their hands on the table, their eyes intent on McQuade's face.

"Take them off," McQuade ordered. "Like the law says."

Billy Ford said, "Listen, I can handle this."

"Then take their guns."

"Do what he says, Billy," Appell said. "Do it!"

The deputy hesitated, then wiped a hand across his mouth. In that motion the red-headed cowhand pushed himself to his feet, his right hand grabbing for his six-gun as he came up. "You take your bloody law and—"

McQuade's open right hand shot out, and he jammed four big stiff fingers into the redhead's stomach. The cowhand grunted and snapped forward like a closing jacknife. McQuade grabbed his shirt with his left hand and spun him around, while his right reached down and slapped the man's .44 into his palm.

The steel barrel leveled off across the table, covering both seated men. McQuade had acted so fast that the well-dressed man hadn't moved, but was still sitting with his hands flat on the top. The second cowhand, taller and thinner than the redhead, had started to drop his right hand, but now he returned it to the table. He rubbed his stubbled jaw nervously and looked into McQuade's hard eyes.

"Hey, there's no need for this," he whined. "Red was only funnin'."

"What's your name?"

"Jessup. Bob Jessup. Look, we was just havin' a game with the drummer here. Red's just had too much to drink."

"Hand your belt to the deputy," McQuade said. He added to the well-dressed man, "Put yours on the table. Careful now."

Jessup unbuckled his gunbelt and held it out for Billy Ford to take. "Look, me and Red are tryin' for jobs with Carson's show. I'll take Red. I'll keep him in our room till Carson gets in."

McQuade pushed the redhead, doubled over and gasping for air, toward the deputy. "Lock the big mouth up." He didn't take his eyes off the drummer. "I said on the table, mister."

"What is this?" Calem Voci questioned. "I didn't do anythin'."

McQuade ignored that. He turned to Appell. "Mayor, I've decided to start right now. You can give me that badge."

"Of course," said Appell, surprised. "But I left it in the office."

"We'll go over now," McQuade said. He reached across the table carefully and unbuttoned Voci's coat front. A bone-handled Starr .44 jutted from the waistband of his trousers. McQuade pulled it out and kept it in his hand. "This what you're selling, mister?"

Voci's dark features didn't change. "Harnesses and bridles are my line. I'll be doin' two thousand dollars' worth of business with Carson. You can't expect me to carry that kind of money without some protection."

"If you've got business with Carson, you do it down at the siding," McQuade told him, and then to the cowhand named Jessup, "Soon as I'm sworn in, I'm coming back. I want you out of town, too."

McQuade straightened and turned, then walked into the hotel lobby. Mayor Appell caught up with him and put a hand on McQuade's arm.

"That salesman didn't cause any trouble," he said. "He didn't even try for that gun."

"I've seen wanteds on that drummer, Mayor. His name's Calem Voci."

Appell's face stiffened. "Calem Voci!" His thumb and forefinger rubbed at the full flesh along his jawbone while he glanced back into the saloon. Voci had already left the wall table. "He said he only wants to see Carson. There doesn't have to be trouble."

"Not unless a gunman like Voci tries staying, Mayor."

"But—"

"But nothing, Mayor," McQuade pulled open the screen door and started onto the porch. "You hired me to keep this town clean. That's just what I intend to do."

3

INSIDE HIS HOTEL ROOM CALEM VOCI pulled a horse-hide valise and a Henry carbine from beneath the bed. He opened the valise and took out the double gunbelt that was hidden under his soiled clothes. One holster was empty. The other held the twin of the bone-handled Starr .44 McQuade had taken from him. Voci drew the six-gun and rotated the drum to check its load.

The door to the adjoining room opened, and Jessup came in. He held his saddle roll balanced on his shoulder. "What do we do, Voc? Wait outside town 'til English lets us know any change in plans?"

"We can't change plans. Jake Clinton wouldn't get close to the bank now. He wouldn't even get them cows into place before McQuade spotted him."

"We can stop Jake. We can get out and wait with Frenchy." Jessup's talk ceased at the knock on the door. Voci dropped the revolver into the valise and closed it.

"Who is it?" Voci asked.

"Me, Gruber."

Voci moved quickly and pulled back the door. Gruber stepped past him and gazed from the valise to the Henry rifle. "McQuade'll pick you up for havin' that gun. I'll take it down the side way."

"No need to take it any place," Voci said, opening the valise. Carefully, he rearranged the gunbelt and clothing, then laid the six-gun on top.

Gruber stared at him. "Mr. English doesn't want you facin' McQuade alone."

"The hell with English," Voci snarled. "Him and his fool idea of goin' after McQuade in the open." He closed the valise and lifted it with his left hand. He let one grip slip from his fingers far enough so he could reach the Starr. "English's damned fool idea of me dressin' up in

20

these dude clothes. If I had my guns on, I'd've killed McQuade before he could pull Red in front of him."

Gruber said, "Wait five minutes. I'll get Mr. English."

Voci shook his head. "McQuade'll be up here in five minutes. You get back to the saloon and try slowin' him down."

He walked to the window and stood looking out through the long white curtains. McQuade still hadn't left the marshal's office. If he figured right, McQuade's taking his time meant he didn't want a gunfight right now—and that was what Voci planned on, what he depended on. He turned and said to Jessup, "Tell the clerk I'm checkin' out. Be sure he knows I'm leavin'."

"Look, Voci," Gruber said worriedly. "We got you in to take care of McQuade. I'm not supposed to handle anything like this."

"You slow him down," Voci snapped. "Do some of that talkin' you're so damn good at. But you'd better help get his attention away from me."

Voci turned his back on Gruber and walked to the bed. He lifted the Henry, then returned to the window and stood the rifle barrel-down behind the curtain.

"You both make it sound good," he said. "One clear shot. That's all I need to take care of McQuade."

Dan McQuade pinned the marshal's badge on his shirt and began buckling his gunbelt around his waist. Mayor Appell, who had been standing close to the doorway ever since he'd sworn in McQuade, saw that word of the trouble had already spread, for men had begun to appear in windows and doorways along Union, all staring either toward the hotel or the jail.

Appell ducked back so he couldn't be seen. For a few seconds he kept silent, watching McQuade tie down his holster.

"Marshal, we never had a gunfight while Ben Ford wore that badge," he said. "I don't want one today."

"I don't either," McQuade answered. He'd finished thonging the Colt, and he brushed his coat open and dropped his hand to judge its hang. Satisfied, he was buttoning his blue serge when Billy Ford came out of the cell block.

The deputy wet his lips and watched McQuade uncertainly. Finally he said, "I'll go over with you."

21

"I'll do this alone, kid."

"I'm no kid. I'm your deputy." Billy returned McQuade's determined look. He was several inches shorter than McQuade, but his body was thicker. At twenty-one there was still a suggestion of boyishness to his square pale face, and his disappointment and anger over needing help in the saloon were nakedly apparent in his honest eyes. "I'll go with you."

"No. You don't face a killer like Voci first time out. You wait here."

"I'm deputy. If there's trouble, it's my job to take part in it."

Mayor Appell said carefully, "That's right, Marshal. Especially because of the people."

"Who said anything about people?"

Appell shrugged. "Nobody. But if it wasn't clear the people have to see the law working, you wouldn't be going after Voci. Billy should be a part of it if he's going to have any strength."

McQuade stared solemnly at the deputy. "All right. But stay ready. Don't expect Voci to give any warning if he wants trouble." He glanced toward the sound of footsteps beyond the door.

He saw a tall, neat-looking man with dust cuffs over the sleeves of his white shirt move past the window and then step inside. He was about McQuade's age, with heavy brows above deep-set eyes. He looked from Appell to McQuade and said quietly, "I was told there was going to be a gunfight. Is that right?"

Appell answered first. "Not exactly, George." He glanced at McQuade and explained, "George English runs the *Tribune*. You can talk to him."

A reflective hardness lurked around McQuade's eyes. George English—he recalled how Ann had said the name. He nodded to the newspaperman. "The mayor will give you the story."

English asked pointedly, "Is a gunfight necessary?" He watched McQuade, his face definite.

"That isn't up to me, Mr. English."

"There might be an easier way of handling this," English suggested, his stare shifting to Appell. "Mayor, would you be willing to talk to that drummer?"

"It won't do any good to talk," McQuade told him.

22

"Voci's made up his mind by this time. Talk won't change it."

"I'd be willing to go over with the mayor," English offered. "I'll do anything to keep our town peaceful."

"Then stay here and let me handle this," McQuade said.

He went out onto the walk and hesitated for a moment to glance across the broad grass flat that stretched west beyond the Platte River, wishing he'd decided to wait out there until Saturday. Some of the onlookers moved forward as he stepped down to the street. It wouldn't be long before they'd begin following him into the hotel saloon, press against the windows or block the doorways and get in his way. McQuade's face remained wooden, but worry grew within him.

Beside him, Billy Ford mumbled, "That cowhand, Jessup. He just went into the livery."

Nodding, McQuade said before he started up the hotel steps, "You stay clear."

"I'll be all right."

"Stay clear," McQuade repeated emphatically. "Voci isn't any drunk cowhand looking for a fight. If he wants trouble, he could start shooting as soon as we step inside."

Tom Gruber, standing with the men grouped opposite the back-bar mirror, cursed obscenely when he saw McQuade crossing the porch. "Look at that," he remarked loudly. "He's damn well ready to push that drummer into a gunfight. You look and see if he ain't."

The small talk that broke out died the instant McQuade pushed through the batwings. His hard, tight eyes ran across the faces, then to the lobby doorway. McQuade started around the tables near him, past the men at the bar.

Gruber stepped in front of the watching men. "Hey, Marshal!" he called. "Why don't you give that drummer a break? He didn't do nothin'."

McQuade kept his eyes on the lobby. "Who's that man?" he asked Billy over his shoulder.

"Gruber. Tom Gruber. He was deputy under my father. After the council hired you, he quit."

"Shut him up."

"He's only talkin'. He can't hurt you."

"His big mouth'll let Voci know we're coming. Shut him."

"See here, Marshal," Gruber shouted, "I'm talking to you." He'd left the others and had started for the lobby doorway. One of the men behind him laughed, and Gruber moved faster. "This town needs business from the drummers, Marshal. We're putting on Carson's show partly t' get more business here."

"Get back," McQuade warned. The words were low-spoken, but Gruber's expression showed he'd heard them.

Gruber reached the doorway first and kept talking loudly. "It's a rotten shame they got a gun-happy lawman to take Ben Ford's place. But you still ain't got no right to—"

McQuade's left hand rose in a short uppercut to the jaw. Gruber tried to pull away, but the blow landed solidly. Gruber grunted, staggered and fell back.

McQuade grabbed Gruber's shirt front and jerked the round mustached face close to his own. "Keep shut and clear of me," he ordered, his words low and cold. He shoved out hard, smacking Gruber's bulk against the bar. Then McQuade swung around and stepped into the lobby.

The clerk behind the registration desk stared, bug-eyed.

"Had any check-outs?" McQuade asked.

"Yes, two. That cowhand. And that drummer's leavin', too." He shifted uncomfortably and flicked his eyes at the staircase as a boot scuffed on the landing.

Calem Voci had started down the stairs, holding his valise in his left hand and keeping his right hand intentionally well clear of his side.

"I'm not carryin', McQuade," he said. "You can see."

"You're checking out."

Voci's swarthy features didn't change when he nodded. "I'm a drummer. I've got a right to see the town authorities about this."

"You'll see them outside town, just like you'll see Carson."

McQuade watched Voci closely. He could hear quiet conversation begin among the watchers beyond the saloon doorway. They believed Voci had backed down, and only a few moments passed before they began pressing into the lobby. Billy Ford walked ahead of Voci. He pulled the screen door open and held it for Voci to go outside first.

Billy looked around at McQuade and grinned widely. "That was so easy."

"Watch it!" McQuade yelled. "Watch it!" He moved as

he talked. His left arm came up and shoved hard into Billy's chest, cutting off the deputy's words, slamming him violently into the wall.

Dumfounded, Billy heard the sudden fearful yells of the spectators. He regained his balance and straightened, watching McQuade's right hand streak down and come up with his six-gun.

Gunfire blasted through the lobby, three shots that sounded almost as one. McQuade's hat was torn from his head, and Calem Voci's body stiffened at the impact of McQuade's bullets. Jerked around, he was sent sprawling through the open doorway and landed face down on the porch.

Billy stepped away from the wall and grabbed at McQuade's arm. "You killed him! You just threw down on him and started shooting!"

"Turn him over," McQuade said. He bent and picked up his hat.

The deputy didn't move. He took a deep breath and glared into McQuade's tight-jawed face. "Ann didn't want me to be your deputy. I can see why."

"Turn him over."

Billy walked onto the porch, oblivious of the men who crowded in behind him. Up and down Union talk was going on, and boots clomped along the walks. Billy crouched and rolled Voci's body onto its side. The right arm was twisted awkwardly, the hand covered by the valise. Two wide red stains dotted his shirt, both within an inch of the heart.

McQuade kicked the valise aside. Billy saw the bone-handled .44, one spent cartridge hanging halfway out of the drum, still gripped in the motionless hand. A bitter bile taste rose in Billy's mouth, and he swallowed.

"I didn't see, Marshal."

"Get him down to the coroner's," McQuade said. He'd already taken two bullets from his belt, and he slid them into the empty chambers. "Then come over to the office."

McQuade stepped down off the porch. Men, women and children passed him, crowding in around the steps. Others came only as far as the middle of the street or watched from in front of stores and houses. Rapid talk filled the walks, nervous, high-pitched chatter.

One woman touched McQuade's arm and stared into his

eyes, her face scared, questioning. "Why? Why in our town?" she asked shrilly. "We don't want gunfights here."

Without answering, McQuade moved past her toward the jail. He'd taken just two steps when he noticed that the cowhand named Jessup had come out of the livery barn on a black gelding. McQuade halted and watched Jessup pull the animal in at the rear of the crowd and then sit his saddle rigidly while he stared blankly down at the dead man.

Jessup's stare shifted to McQuade. For a second McQuade thought the rider was going to come toward him. But Jessup, his face still without any readable expression, backed his mount and headed it westward.

"Dan, have you seen Stevie?"

McQuade turned to face Ann Heath. She was out of breath, her cheeks flushed from running. "He was playing in the yard. When I came out he was gone."

"No," he said. "But there are a lot of kids out here."

He glanced through the crowd. Ann started past him, and he touched her arm. "It's all over, Ann. If he's out here, he didn't get hurt."

She jerked her arm away. The town was exactly what she knew it would be after a gunfight—people grouped all along the center, some of the men, excited and fascinated, following those who were carrying the dead man toward the undertaker's. Just like six years ago, when she'd run out to find her husband lying face down in Tombstone's main street. Now she could think only of her son.

"There's Steve," she heard McQuade say. "To the left of the hotel porch. With two other boys."

Ann nodded and started ahead again. McQuade said, "That gunfight, Ann. It couldn't be helped."

She looked at him, her fear changed to an unbelieving stare. McQuade's nerves tightened. There had been a slight chance of hope in the yard, but he knew even that had vanished completely.

"You haven't been here one hour," she told him bitterly, and gave him no chance to answer. She moved into the crowd, her lips again compressed in a thin, worried line.

The excitement had gone through the whole town. Everywhere she heard noisy, rapid talk. Women stood

26

beside their husbands and held their children close to them. "He was a gunfighter named Voci," a man on the hotel porch was yelling. "He drew on the new marshal."

"Had a gun hid in his bag," another added. "Got a shot off, too. Millett's diggin' the slug outta the wall."

"I don't like it," a third said. "Ain't no reason for a shootout here."

Ann reached her son and put her hand on Stevie's shoulder. Wide-eyed, the boy stared up into her face. "They had a gunfight," he told her. "The marshal shot a killer."

"Come home, Stevie. I told you not to leave the yard."

Stevie glanced at the other boys. "I want to stay. I want to watch."

Her hand dropped to his arm and tightened. "I don't want you out here."

"Aw, Mommy."

"Do what your mother tells you," said George English from behind them. "This is no place for you, Steven."

Ann's eyes met English's. "You shouldn't be out here, either," he said gently. He leaned close to the boy. "You don't want your mother to be in any danger, do you?"

Disappointment covered the small face, but Stevie shook his head. English took Ann's elbow and guided her toward the alleyway to the right of the jail. He could feel her arm shaking under his hand.

"I'll go to the house with you," he said.

They reached the walk. English slowed and asked quietly, "You're certain you're all right?"

"Yes. I'll take Stevie in." She hesitated and looked into his face. "Thank you, George. You're so good, so understanding." Her gaze moved to the door of the marshal's office and returned to English. "I'd like to talk to you later. When Stevie is in bed."

"I'll stop by. Soon as I lock up the paper."

"No. I'll come to your office," she said. "The Hobson girl will sit for me."

English nodded, then remained motionless until the woman and boy turned into the alley. After they disappeared, he stepped off the walk and crossed Union to where Gruber stood on the hotel porch. Gruber looked nervous and worried. He opened his mouth when English reached him, then shut it again.

27

"Just walk," English said. "Make it look normal. Down the side of the hotel."

"Sure. Sure, Mr. English."

They had traveled only as far as the edge of the porch before Gruber blurted, "I tried to stop Voci, Mr. English. He wouldn't—"

"All right. It's unfortunate, but it doesn't spoil anything. Just shut up."

At the alleyway English turned in, but he halted once he was within the deep shadows between the buildings. Overhead the prairie night had come fast, stars winking and multiplying in the blackening sky. Two hundred yards beyond the foot of the alley, they could still make out Jessup. Horse and rider were barely visible, almost blending with the thick darkness of the flat, but both were clear enough for English to be certain where Jessup was heading.

"He'll tell Clinton," English said finally. "We keep the same plan, only Frenchy will do the shooting from his room. You'll tell him."

"I will, Mr. English." Gruber went to step onto the boardwalk.

"Not now. He's not here, you fool." English's sharp voice made the words a command. "Get back to the crowd and keep the talk going against McQuade."

Gruber glanced out at the street. "McQuade won't stand for talk like Billy Ford," he complained, rubbing his jaw. "It won't work with him."

"Not with him. With the crowd. Just the talk about the gunmen who'd like to see McQuade dead. You gripe enough and the people will be ready for anything Saturday."

"I'm not sure, Mr.—"

"I know," English said, low and cold. Frowning, he eyed the brick building across Union that had *Farmington National Bank* printed on its long front window.

"You know, Gruber," English said shortly, "I spent six months planning and getting things set up for just ten minutes on Saturday." His voice had lost its sharpness, but it was still deadly. "Now it's so close, nothing or nobody is going to spoil it. McQuade—you, nobody."

He stared directly into Gruber's round face and saw the corners of the moustached mouth twitch. "Remember that when you talk out there, Gruber."

4

That drummer was pushed into a shootout. And Mayor Appell's the one to blame. He hired McQuade."

Tom Gruber's loud voice had caused a restless quiet to come over the townspeople. Gruber, one outstretched arm pointed at Appell, stood on the edge of the hotel porch. His confident posture was in striking contrast to the mayor's stiffness at the rear of the crowd.

"Voci was a wanted gunman," Appell answered. "You would have let him stay, I suppose?"

"That's right. Just like Ben Ford would've done. I'd've let him get his business done and—"

"And do anything else he wanted. That's about it, Gruber."

A man swore, and the word grew into talk, which murmured through the watchers. Even the women joined in, speaking softly to their husbands. Somehow, after the chatter died, uncertainty was left behind. No one mentioned it, or asked questions or commented on Gruber's outburst. The gap of silence was filled by the sound of feet moving as the crowd split up.

"Anyway, I'm sure of one thing," Gruber called, trying to keep their attention. "There's plenty people who liked how Ben Ford kept things. They won't cotton to a gunfighter wearin' Ben's badge." He waved one arm, including all the listeners. "Everybody knows that Voci had friends who'll hear 'bout this."

"You stop that," Appell said. "You've got no right spreading talk like that."

"I'll say what I think's right. There ain't no law that gun-happy McQuade can force on me for it." Gruber cursed, swung around and stomped across the porch into the saloon.

Four of the watchers followed Gruber. Appell, noticing them and the disgruntled faces near him, took a step toward the porch. George English's hand on his sleeve held him up.

"You booted that one," said English. "You should be smarter than to argue out in the street."

"George, everyone realizes Gruber's done nothing but make trouble since we hired McQuade."

"What do you expect him to do after we took the marshal's job away from him? Right now I think we'd better get Henry Stillwell and let McQuade see the council is with him."

Appell's face clouded. "I'm not sure about Henry. You know how he feels about McQuade."

Nodding, English smiled. "We outvoted Stillwell the last time. We can handle him now. I still believe the best thing we ever did was hiring McQuade to marshal our town."

Through the office window McQuade watched Appell and English cross Union to the bank. He hadn't been able to hear what had gone on between Gruber and the mayor, but he had caught the mention of his name. He'd seen the silent, furtive glances the people had given the jail when they'd walked past. That was enough for McQuade to know just how the citizens of Farmington felt.

He shook his head wearily. He couldn't even have the few days he needed with these people. They wouldn't understand if the Clintons came, no more than Ann had understood. And the Clintons would come, once word of the gunfight was spread by the passengers on the next westbound train.

McQuade shook his head again, watching as Billy Ford rounded the corner of Cross Street. Voci's bullet had come too close to killing him, all because the deputy hadn't listened before they'd gone into the saloon. McQuade remained close to the window until the deputy reached the boardwalk. Then he stepped back to the desk.

"Whatever made you want to be a lawman?" McQuade asked the moment Billy came inside.

Billy stared blankly at him. "I—well, my father was always a lawman."

"Your father." McQuade's eyes went over the younger man, and he shook his head. "You figure you take a badge just to keep it in the family?"

"No. It isn't that. I've always wanted to be a lawman. Ever since I was a kid I've hung around this office. I'd stay as close to my father as I could. Sometimes he took me with him when he went out."

"Your father never went out after a gunman like Voci."

Billy's face tightened. "He ran a good town. A safe one."

"He was lucky." McQuade spoke flatly, without malice. "And you were lucky to see only the good side of wearing that badge. I know your father never had a shootout all the time he was marshal. But it isn't always that way. You wear a badge, sooner or later you'll bump into a Calem Voci. If your father never had a gunfight, he wouldn't have walked away from Voci's gun."

"He had a way of handlin' men like Voci."

"You saw me try giving Voci a break. And what happened?" McQuade took a deep breath, held down his voice. "You know the nice quiet side of the law. Good. Then you'd do better to find a marshal who'll sit by and let killers like Voci walk their streets. You better resign here and find a town like that."

"No. This is my home town. I'll stay."

"Not if you pull another boner you won't." He glanced sidelong at the three men who'd appeared in the doorway— Mayor Appell, English and a gray-bearded man who wore a black suit and fedora. He halted behind the others and regarded McQuade with level, officious eyes.

Appell said, "We represent the council, Marshal. You know the editor. This is Henry Stillwell from the bank. We felt we should come over and show that we're behind you."

English nodded to Appell's words. The banker raised one hand toward his fedora but stopped, watching McQuade with a strained, thoughtful look.

He said, "There will have to be an inquest, McQuade."

"That's legal procedure, Mr. Stillwell."

"Yes, I know. Yet, it's unfortunate right now." His glance took in the others and returned to McQuade. "Do you think the inquest can be put off until Saturday? Until after the Wild West Show leaves?"

"Inquests usually take place right away. This one should be held by tomorrow at the latest."

English said, "It would be better for us to wait until late Saturday. There will be some businessmen coming in tomorrow or Saturday morning, some people from the railroad and most of the farmers, too. It wouldn't be good to be holding an inquest. You understand."

Stillwell cleared his throat. "We're not a wild town, McQuade. We want the railroad people to see that. Postponing the inquest until the show leaves would still serve justice."

"If that's the case," said McQuade, "I'd leave it up to the coroner."

Appell said, "Good, that's good." He sucked in a deep breath and concentrated on watching Stillwell.

"Then we'll leave it at that," the banker said. "I'll talk to the judge." He turned to leave.

McQuade asked, "Mr. Stillwell, do you keep a lot of money in your bank?"

The banker stopped and stared back at McQuade as though he didn't completely understand. "I don't see what that has to do with you."

"Gunmen like Calem Voci don't happen to be in just any town," McQuade explained. "He specialized in banks. I can't see why he'd sit around acting like a drummer for nothing."

Stillwell shook his head. "I wouldn't know. That man was in town a whole day. He never came into the bank."

"Which means nothing, Mr. Stillwell."

At that the banker's expression changed and became cold and officious again. "It could mean he was a man who hoped to make a new life at being a salesman."

McQuade started to answer, but Appell spoke up. "Henry, that drummer drew on the marshal first. No legitimate salesman would try to kill a lawman. Not just because he was ordered out of town."

"That's what I think," English said. "You know how I feel about this."

"Henry, we don't want any trouble among ourselves," Appell added.

"I want the facts set straight," Stillwell told him. He stared into McQuade's eyes. "We had quite a few meetings before you were hired. Those of us who wanted a local man were outvoted."

"Mayor Appell told me about the vote," McQuade said.

Stillwell let out a slow breath. "I wanted you to know," he said curtly. "And you can forget any idea that Voci was after the farmers' money. Most of what I had on hand went out for spring loans. That money won't come in until after harvest."

McQuade nodded his head slowly. When he didn't speak, Stillwell swung around and went outside. English smiled sympathetically at McQuade as he left. Appell started to follow, then hesitated.

"I'll have you meet the other council members tomorrow, Marshal. We're having a dance at night. They'll all be there, so you'll get to know people fast enough."

"Good, Mayor."

McQuade moved behind Appell to the door and stood looking out. Beyond the walk, the dusty street was almost white in the bright floodlight beam of a full moon and the countless stars. Now that the day's heat had died, the night seemed almost chill. McQuade breathed in deeply and rubbed his chin as he watched the mayor run along the road to catch up with Stillwell.

He could say no more to these men. He could do no more. He'd seen traces of doubt on each man's face. In a way, their uncertainty was as much of a threat as Calem Voci had been on the staircase. But, with Voci, it had just been a matter of waiting for him to make his play, then making positive his own gun was faster, surer. With these men, McQuade knew only that he could be really sure of nothing.

Behind him, Billy Ford shifted his feet. "I usually check Union at suppertime," he said.

McQuade looked around. "I wasn't just talking. I'm not sure why Voci was here. It's your neck."

"It's my neck then."

"Okay," McQuade said, nodding. "You watch stupid tricks like getting between my gun and Voci's."

"I didn't think he had a gun."

"You'd better start thinking. Never shift your eyes from a prisoner. Even if he's just a drunk, keep watching. You're just as dead if a drunk decides to try his luck." He gestured with his right hand, taking in the entire town. "And don't let me hear you *ask* people to obey the law. You *tell* them."

He watched the deputy and waited for Billy to answer. Then McQuade stepped to the gunrack and lifted a ten-gauge Greener shotgun from its place.

"If there's ever any real trouble, this is what you use.

33

Not many gunmen'd face being blasted with this." He moved to the desk and opened the two top drawers before he found a box of shotgun shells. He broke the shotgun, loaded the chambers and held the weapon out to Billy.

"Take it into that saloon two blocks down. Ask the owner if we can keep it under the bar."

Billy was doubtful. "There really isn't any reason. My father never had to hide guns."

"When I see a wanted gunman registered at that hotel, I know I'd better be ready," McQuade said. He shoved the weapon into the deputy's hand and forced him to accept it. "I'll leave one in the newspaper office and another in the hotel. That way we'll have the whole street covered."

Without a word, Billy went outside. McQuade lifted two more shotguns from the rack. After he'd loaded them, he took one in each hand and stepped onto the walk.

Loungers gathered on the hotel porch leaned forward in their chairs at the sight of McQuade carrying two shotguns. One was Tom Gruber. The mustached man's voice carried in the quiet, clearly audible to McQuade.

"There. You look there. You tell me if thet ain't lookin' fer trouble."

McQuade paid no attention. He walked slowly toward the *Tribune* building.

For the fourth time during the last half-hour, Bob Jessup pulled up his black gelding in the scrub willow that lined the high right bank of the Platte. He cocked his head and listened. He paid no attention to the fireflies and mosquitoes that hummed around him; he just sat tense and motionless, straining his ears to catch any hint of noise on his backtrail.

He'd ridden hard since leaving Farmington and had put as much distance as possible between himself and McQuade. He wasn't sure how much McQuade knew, what he suspected, but he did know that he would come hunting once he learned the real reason Voci had been in town.

Finally, Jessup kneed his horse forward again. He pushed the black hard until he saw the flicker of a campfire in a cluster of cottonwoods ahead. He reined in, dismounted, then drew the animal on the bridle after him while he approached the campfire carefully.

He'd taken only ten steps before the sharp voice came clearly to him. "Stop right there. Keep them hands high."

Jessup said, "Hold it! It's me, Frenchy! Jessup!"

Boots scuffed on the grass, and the huge shape of a man, Colt .44 in hand, appeared from the closest cottonwood. The black-bearded giant, shoulders and chest bulging under his checkered shirt, glared from under his sombrero.

"You should be in town, Jessup. What in hell you doin' here?"

"I couldn't stay in Farmington." Quickly, he told what had happened. "And McQuade is holdin' Red on a gun charge. The only thing I could do was get out here and stop Jake from goin' in."

Frenchy Pohl grunted and shifted his weight. "What 'bout Voci's rifle. McQuade got that?"

"He didn't see it. He didn't go up to Voci's room."

"He will." Frenchy swore. "You shouldn't've run. All McQuade's gotta do is find that rifle and he'll start askin' questions. He learns I drove that wagon in, he'll go to my place and find how I got things set up."

"Look, Frenchy. He got my gun. There was nothin' I could do but get out."

One big hand waved Jessup quiet. "Plenty that can be done." He paused, began to unbuckle his gunbelt. "I get in fast enough, I can cover things up."

"What if McQuade sees you?"

"What in hell can he do? I'm jest a cowhand lookin' fer a job with that Wild West Show. I'm not packin' a gun." He held out the gunbelt to Jessup. "I'll be back 'fore Jake gets here with the cattle."

"You shouldn't go, Frenchy. Goin' in without anythin', you're takin' a big chance."

"I got somethin'." The giant's sure, bovine features didn't change, but a grin cracked his thick lips when he bent over and reached inside the top of his right boot. His hand came up with the long-bladed Mexican knife he had hidden there.

"You jest wait here for Jake Clinton," he said. "I'll be back."

5

George English said "That's why you decided to wait until Saturday's train."

Ann Heath nodded slowly. "I had to be sure, George." Since she'd entered the newspaper office, she'd stood near the desk. Now she moved across the room, close to English. "Dan was so good to me when my husband was killed, so thoughtful and kind. He even had a woman stay with me until Stevie was born. And after. I've always felt guilty, leaving as I did."

"I understand." English's eyes held hers, and he added, "You won't have to worry about ever coming back here."

She started to speak, but he raised his hand and touched her lips. "No. It's better if I sell the paper. I was waiting only until you were certain, and then—" He stiffened, looked toward the front of the room as the street door opened.

Ann turned and saw Dan McQuade step through the doorway. She stared at the two shotguns he carried.

McQuade stopped short. "Oh, I didn't see you."

"It's all right," Ann said. "I was just going."

McQuade moved aside awkwardly, saying nothing as English walked onto the porch with Ann. He couldn't see her expression, but he felt ridiculous breaking in on them that way. If he hadn't been watching the street so carefully, and every alleyway he passed, he might have seen she was inside.

When English came back, his handsome face was unreadable. "Ann's leaving on Saturday's train," he said simply. "I hope you understand."

McQuade nodded. He envied English, but he couldn't hate him. What had happened wasn't English's fault. It wasn't anyone's fault, unless it was his own.

He laid one of the shotguns on the desk. "I wanted your

permission to leave this in here," he said. "Where it'll be handy."

"Why, yes. If you believe it's necessary."

Concern marked English's manner. McQuade sensed it, and he smothered his sudden urge to laugh. This man, above all others, had no reason to worry about him. He opened the closet beside the door. "Do you keep this locked?"

"It won't be." English's expression deepened as he watched McQuade stand the weapon in the closet. "I didn't want to say anything in your office. Could you have been wrong about that salesman?"

"He was Calem Voci, Mr. English."

"I can't quite understand this." He pointed to the type form on the desk. "He came in like all the other salesmen. He took an ad for the harness and bridle firm he represented. I talked to him. He claimed he'd contacted Carson about outfitting the horses in the show."

McQuade studied the ad and said shortly, "It was Voci. And he drew on me."

"I know. Still, I can't understand his taking an ad if he meant any trouble."

"You don't figure men like Voci. You just watch and see what they try to do." He stepped back to the door. "Obliged, Mr. English."

English stood in the open doorway and felt himself tighten as he watched McQuade cross toward the hotel. He had no worry where Ann was concerned, but he couldn't help thinking McQuade suspected more than he'd shown. That would account for his planting weapons where they'd be accessible at all times. It was exactly what English would have done if he wore a marshal's badge. He'd learned to have more respect for McQuade.

English shut the door and opened the closet. He lifted the shotgun, broke it and took out the two shells. Carefully he replaced the weapon in the exact position McQuade had left it. Then he walked quickly out the back door.

Inside the Granger Hotel the chandeliers had been turned up, lighting the lobby brighter than daytime. This small thin-faced clerk shifted uncomfortably when McQuade laid the shotgun on the desk counter.

"Well, I don't know," he began to protest. "I can shoot

37

it, but I don't think it's safe to have a shotgun out in the open."

"It'll be under the counter," McQuade said. "You won't be handling it anyway. I will." Seeing the old man's slight nod, he added, "That room Voci had. If it's all right with you, I'll hire it."

The clerk's nod became more pronounced. He grinned as he took a key from the rack and handed it to McQuade. "Number Twenty-two, to the right of the landing."

When McQuade took the key and went up the stairs, Millett carefully lifted the heavy weapon, then leaned over to slide it under the counter. He glanced up when the front door opened. George English had entered and was coming to the desk.

English stopped opposite the desk. "I saw Marshal McQuade come in here, didn't I, Mr. Millett?"

"He's upstairs. He took the room that gunman had."

"Oh. I thought there might be something interesting there for the paper," English said off-handedly. His eyes went to the staircase. "You were in there. How about Voci's belongings? Did he have much with him?"

Millett shook his head. "Only a valise full of dirty clothes. And two empty holsters."

"No other weapons? I'd think a gunman would have more than his revolvers with him."

"Nothin' that I seen," the clerk told him. "If there is, I reckon the marshal'll find it."

The newspaperman nodded and glanced once more toward the stairs. McQuade would find the Henry rifle Voci had hidden up there. He'd start asking questions and looking around. There were some things English knew he'd better check himself.

"Thanks, Mr. Millett," he said. "I'll get the rest of the facts from the marshal later." He stepped away from the desk and walked casually out of the lobby.

Dan McQuade's eyes covered everything, from the doorway of the narrow, high-ceilinged hotel room to the curtained windows. Voci's valise lay on the bed placed against the far wall. Along the left was a dresser and wardrobe. A table, holding a basin and pitcher, and two cane-backed chairs took up most of the remaining space.

McQuade emptied the valise and saw that it contained

38

soiled clothing and a gunbelt and holsters. Opening every drawer in the dresser, he found only some stockings and a dirty white shirt. The wardrobe held nothing.

He stood in the center of the room, looking at the articles on the bed, the empty wardrobe and the dresser drawers lined with old sheets of newspaper.

Then he saw the shadow of the rifle behind the curtain.

He dropped the soiled white shirt on the bed and, pulling back the curtain, lifted the weapon. It was a long-barreled Henry, fully loaded. The way it had been leaned against the wall, the stock had hidden a box of shells at the edge of the window sill. The top of the box had been ripped off so the cartridges could be picked out easily.

A picture was coming now, but it wasn't quite clear— the absence of any boxed goods or harness equipment Voci was supposed to be selling; the Henry and ammunition; Voci's attempt to stay in Farmington at any cost . . .

Downstairs at the desk, McQuade asked the clerk if Voci had come into town with the cowhands who'd been in the card game.

"No. He was alone. No, no—he wasn't either. He had his driver with him."

"Driver?"

The clerk nodded. "A cowboy. Big man. He drove the drummer's wagon. Left it behind the livery barn."

"This cowhand live here?"

Again the bony head nodded. "He took one of the rooms over the livery. I saw him there this mornin'."

"Thanks," McQuade said. He placed the key on the counter and started across the lobby.

George English had circled wide around the two blocks between the hotel and the livery stable so he wouldn't be seen opening the barn's back door. English cursed the brightness of the almost full moon. He'd have a hard time explaining why he was out here like this. It was all McQuade would need to start seeing through things. But, if he didn't make certain Frenchy's gun was hidden, McQuade would know tonight something had been set up.

It would be a simple matter for McQuade once he had Frenchy's gun, too. He'd definitely prove there was a real danger to Henry Stillwell, and there'd be absolutely no chance for Clinton and his men to get inside the bank.

The mixed, pungent smell of hay, coal smoke and horse droppings was thick in English's nostrils as he edged past the rows of stalls to the ladderlike stairs. He could hear Seth Perrault and one of his friends talking and laughing out front. English went up the stairs slowly. He waited until the men outside broke into loud laughter again before he opened the door of Frenchy's room.

Bending his body low, English struck a sulphur match with his thumbnail, then cupped it in his hands so it wouldn't throw a glare. A lone chair stood in front of the window. As the tiny flicker of light covered one corner of the chair, English saw the Winchester .73 that lay flat across the seat.

"The fool," English muttered. "The stupid fool." He blew out the match and picked up the weapon. It was fully loaded. "The stupid, stupid fool."

Outside, the men had stopped their talk. A footstep sounded on the gravel of the work area. English slid along the wall and peered out. McQuade, Voci's Henry in his right hand, was still a good forty feet from the barn. His tall figure was a perfect target, etched clearly in the background of the street lamps.

English, dropping the temptation to shoot, started out of the room. Killing McQuade now would be a mistake. He'd been promised to Jake Clinton, and, above all, English meant to keep that promise.

Neither of the men who were sitting tilted back in chairs near the big double door, smoking, spoke when McQuade stopped.

"There's a cowhand staying in one of your rooms," the lawman said to Seth Perrault. "He drove a wagon loaded with harnesses in here."

"Yep. Name's Frenchy somethin'. He rode out of town 'round eleven this mornin'. Said he'd be back tonight sometime."

McQuade nodded and looked up at the three windows over the doorway. "I'd like to look in his room."

"Cain't let you do that," Seth said, his long thin face serious. "His things are up there."

"I won't touch them." McQuade started inside.

"Look here, I said you couldn't go in." One hand reached out and grabbed at McQuade's shoulder.

McQuade stepped aside and gave the arm a shove that made the hostler pull back. An instantaneous flash of anger came across Seth's face, but the expression dissolved into mixed fear and indignation. Drawing himself up stiffly, he whined, "Look, don't break the door. It's the middle room. It ain't locked."

McQuade, continuing on, lifted the lighted lantern that hung from a nail just beyond the open doorway.

Inside Frenchy's room he noted the position of the chair near the window. He paused beside the chair and held the lantern higher in order to check the entire room.

His eyes ran over a soiled shirt hung on one of the nails driven into the wall, the cotlike bed and the washbowl and pitcher on the bedside table. He caught the shadow of something behind the pitcher, stepped to the table and found a small box of .44 cartridges. Like the box he'd found in Voci's room, the top had been torn off so there'd be no trouble getting out the shells.

McQuade had the almost complete picture even before he walked to the window and looked down along Union. The chair spotted too carefully, the way the window viewed everything between the barn and the hotel—both tied in with Voci's hotel window, which viewed the same area from that direction. Everything was covered—the jail, the bank, every building, every person who'd be in the street.

McQuade nodded his head patiently and doused the lamp before he started down the stairs.

6

For the next forty-five minutes McQuade waited inside the barn doorway, watching the street. Seth Perrault and his companion sat and smoked as usual, but they talked little. Three riders came into town during that time. It wasn't until the third was halfway down Union, both the huge black-bearded rider and claybank clearly visible in the bright moonlight, that Seth glanced around to where McQuade stood.

"That's him," Seth said.

"Let him ride all the way in here."

But the rider didn't come the length of Union. He reined in at the restaurant and climbed down from the saddle. As McQuade walked toward him, he saw the big man wore no gunbelt. And he didn't have a rifle in the saddle boot.

Close now, McQuade asked quietly, "They call you Frenchy? You work for a drummer handling harness goods?"

"I drive for him," Frenchy Pohl said.

McQuade nodded. "I want to look inside the boxes he brought with him."

The giant gave a slight gesture at the hotel. "You'll have to talk to my boss. He owns that stuff."

"The drummer's dead. You open those boxes."

One big hand rose and wiped the corner of the whiskered mouth as Frenchy's eyes flicked to the hotel porch. The loungers there had been listening, and now three of them started across the street. "If there's been trouble, I'm no part of it, mister."

"Then open those boxes. We'll take a few up to your room." McQuade pulled the box of .44 shells from his pocket and held it in his hand where Frenchy could see it.

He watched Frenchy's eyes tighten and saw the huge man wipe his mouth again. McQuade didn't like waiting,

42

but he'd made up his mind about one thing—he'd try to handle this quietly, as the townspeople wanted. He'd give Frenchy his chance to come along willingly, without any rough stuff. But he was going to come along. It was all up to Frenchy.

When Frenchy talked, his voice was calm and flat. "Okay, wagon's out back."

He moved as if to pass McQuade, but after the first step he whirled in a complete turn, bringing his massive right fist around in a vicious hook.

McQuade, having expected something like that, pulled his chin back, wove his broad shoulders clear and moved in on Frenchy. The giant's miss had momentarily thrown him off balance. Before he could recover, McQuade swung out with his right. The blow, landing solidly above the left ear, knocked Frenchy sprawling beneath the hitchrail.

Frenchy's claybank stomped and jerked its head up, trying to pull free of the rail. Talk broke out among the watchers.

Swearing, Frenchy pushed himself away from the horse's hoofs. He got quickly to his feet, rubbing the skin and hair over his ear, his deep-set eyes mean and hot.

"I ain't goin' no place with you, mister," he said. He crouched low, his right arm falling to his leg as he moved.

"He's got a knife!" a man yelled. "Back! He's got a knife!"

The watchers fell into tense silence, those in close pressing back. The boot heels clattered along the boardwalk and the horse's stomping was loud in the silence.

"Your mistake, mister," Frenchy sneered. He threw his right hand out in front of him, revealing the nasty, long-bladed weapon he'd drawn from his boot. He called McQuade an obscene name and lunged forward.

McQuade moved to the left, watching the razor-sharp blade come at him with the cutting edge up, ready to make one wide swipe across his stomach or throat. He held both of his hands wide from his sides, knowing one didn't use his hands against a blade, one didn't kick at it and take a chance on losing balance.

The knife missed by inches. Frenchy cursed, came out of his crouch and charged in again. McQuade backed to the right. The blade slashed past McQuade's stomach, two inches closer than before. Instead of shifting his attack, the giant continued with the wide sweep, nicking McQuade's left hand.

McQuade felt the sharp twitch of pain, then the warm moisture of his own blood. He'd had enough. The importance of showing the townspeople that he wanted to handle Frenchy without any brutality vanished. McQuade danced to the rear three steps, then to the right, his good hand gripping the wounded one to stop the flow of blood.

He heard the high-pitched, excited talk of the spectators, Frenchy's deep, frenzied laughter.

Frenchy stalked in, surer of himself as his arm shot out. McQuade's left flashed up and yanked off his Stetson. His right dropped back and picked his Colt from its holster while he swept the hat down into the blade.

The blade tore in and caught. Frenchy tried to jerk it free for another stab, but McQuade's steel barrel smashed down on the back of his head. Frenchy let out a wild yell and toppled groggily, blood flowing from the gash behind his ear.

The watchers exhaled drawn breaths loudly, gasping in amazed silence. McQuade bent over the huge prostrate body and kicked the knife clear of Frenchy's reach. Frenchy lay prone, dismayed at the suddenness of what had happened. He wiped one hairy arm across his eyes, then moved it back to feel at the bleeding cut.

McQuade took out a white handkerchief and wrapped it around his own hand. He crouched over the giant. "What was Voci here for?"

Frenchy's hazy eyes rolled and focused themselves on McQuade. "He had bridles for Major Carson. That's all I know."

McQuade bent closer to the wide, bearded face. "It was more than that. Why?"

"I don't know, I tell you."

McQuade grabbed Frenchy's shirt and shook him savagely. "You'll tell me or—"

"Hey, don't beat him!" a voice screamed close to McQuade's head. A hand grasped McQuade's shoulder roughly. "He's down! You got no right beating him!"

McQuade turned his body reflexively, throwing a long straight left as he moved. The doubled fist smashed bone and sent the man who'd leaned over his shoulder reeling into the crowd.

It was Gruber. His fat, mustached face twisted with

44

pain as he wiped blood from his lip. "Crazy killer! You crazy killer!"

McQuade straightened. His eyes were on Frenchy, but he was aware of every movement in the crowd. The men gathered together along the walk looked shocked and worried. They didn't understand why he'd used his gun barrel; they felt only growing irritation and anger at seeing a man brutally beaten. Billy Ford had pushed his way through from the rear.

"Break this up," McQuade called to the deputy. "Get them back."

He edged to the left cautiously, making Frenchy stand in front of him. The onlookers were quiet now, and the majority of them had backed away even before Billy got to the hitch-rail. Most of them were standing stiff-legged, visibly afraid to go any closer to McQuade.

McQuade shoved Frenchy ahead of him. "Here," he said as soon as Billy was beside him. "Get him over to the jail." He reached out and grabbed Gruber's arm. "This one, too."

"Why me?" Gruber said, protesting.

"Get going," McQuade snapped, pushing Gruber in beside Frenchy.

Muttered comments started as the two men were taken away. The crowd became a whispering, restless noise of voices, shuffling feet and the rustle of clothing.

"Why in the world's he takin' Gruber in?" someone asked.

"Dunno."

"Gruber didn't do nothin'. He was jest tryin' t' stop him from beatin' that cowhand."

McQuade leaned down and picked the knife and his Stetson from the dirt. The blade had ripped a wide gash from the crown to the brim, and there was a light smear of blood where his hand had held it.

"Too danged bad he didn't cut his gun hand," a man on the restaurant porch said.

"Yeah," another agreed. "We wouldn't have no more trouble like this."

McQuade turned away from the crowd, put his hat on his head and crossed Union to the jail.

George English had seen the fight from start to finish.

All during the time McQuade had waited inside the blacksmith's, English had been watching from the window of his newspaper office. He'd come outside when McQuade had called his first question to Frenchy, and he'd seen how McQuade had baited the big man with the box of shells.

English hardly heard the talk of the crowd. He stared at the groggy way the huge man walked toward the jail. English's forehead wrinkled, his face puzzled. That stumbling, bleeding hulk was Frenchy Pohl, the brute Jake Clinton had said had killed two men with his own bare hands. Frenchy, who could use a knife like an Indian. It had taken only one quick sidestep for McQuade to draw him in and finish him off.

"Did you see that, George?" asked Appell. The mayor's round cheeks were flushed, his eyes worried. "I heard the yells from my store. Did you see the whole thing?"

"Only the end. That cowhand must have pulled a knife on McQuade."

"Why?"

English's eyes traveled across the faces of the men who were standing in the street. Their talk was all against McQuade. English waited until Appell heard some of their remarks before he answered. "I don't know. I think we might've made a mistake, John."

Appell did not answer, and English added, "That's a killing and a knife fight since McQuade got here. Listen to those people."

The mayor bowed his head and looked toward the yellow lamplight that beamed out through the open doorway of the marshal's office. His thumb and forefinger rubbed at the loose flesh along his chin. "I'm going over there," he said finally. "Come on with me."

English touched Appell's arm and said quietly, "Maybe you shouldn't be too hasty. Find out what's going on before you do anything."

"That's just what I intend to do." Appell started off the walk, and George English fell in alongside him.

Billy hadn't put Gruber into a cell yet. Gruber spun around when he heard McQuade's footsteps come through the office into the cell block and rubbed unconsciously at his split lip.

"You got no right lockin' me up, McQuade."

46

McQuade moved past him. "Get back in the office," he said. "Wait there."

"But you've got no right holdin' me."

"Get in there and wait."

Gruber began walking. McQuade stopped beside Billy. In the closest cell, Frenchy was sitting on the bunk, slumped forward a bit, one hand probing carefully at the swollen skin behind his ear. From the last cubicle, the red-headed cowboy watched with his face pressed close to the vertical bars.

"Get over to the livery," McQuade told Billy. "Open up the boxes in Voci's wagon."

"There's only harnesses in there," Frenchy called loudly. "You're makin' all this over nothin'."

"Then we'll open them here," McQuade said, and, looking at the deputy, "Bring three or four back with you."

Billy Ford left. McQuade stepped directly beneath the ceiling lamp and unwrapped the handkerchief from his hand. The knife cut was an inch long, in the fleshy part just below his wrist. But it wasn't deep, and the blood had already coagulated. He wrapped the wound up again and turned to Frenchy.

"What was Voci doing here?"

The huge man's mouth was twisted, ready to curse McQuade, but at the sound of footsteps within the office his expression changed. "He was drummin' harnesses."

McQuade had seen Mayor Appell and English come inside. He paid no attention to them, or to the answer.

"Voci wanted to stay here bad enough to die for it," he said. "If it was just a matter of selling, he could've done it outside town."

Frenchy's raised hand moved over the swelling to the blood that was still seeping from his torn skin. His eyes switched to the office, as though he expected the men in the doorway to come into the cell block.

"Hey," he called to Appell. "You're the mayor, ain't you? I need a doctor."

"The doc'll see you after you talk," said McQuade. "What about Voci?"

"That drummer? I don't know nothin' 'bout him. I was in Omaha lookin' for a job, and he hired me to handle his wagon." He glanced into the office. "Hell, I didn't even like the guy. He was one of them fast-talkin' dudes."

47

"He was Calem Voci, and you know it."

"Calem Voci? Who in hell's Calem Voci?"

Mayor Appell walked past the doors of the cell block. English followed a step behind him.

"Marshal, couldn't we send for the doctor?" Appell said. "This man might not have known he was working for a gunman."

"He knew, Mayor. He knew enough to pull a knife on me."

"You hit me," Frenchy said fast. "I got mad." He'd started to sweat; little drops formed along the ridges of his forehead and rolled down to his black beard. He wiped one cheek with the back of his hand. "Look, I'm sorry. I'll take whatever the judge gives me."

Footsteps sounded beyond the office doorway, and Billy Ford came in carrying a heavy wooden box. Seth Perrault and two other townsmen, carrying similar boxes, followed the deputy into the center of the office.

Billy put his down and lifted off the top. "Only harnesses and bridles in these," he said. "I opened every box. That's all there was."

The others laid their boxes beside the one the deputy had opened. They stood back silently, listening.

"See, I told you, Marsh'l," Frenchy called. "All we was doin' was drummin' that stuff."

Seth Perrault, looking at the other two townsmen, said something in a low voice. All three faces showed doubt concerning McQuade—and anger, too.

"All right," McQuade said to the men. "Leave the boxes here."

"What 'bout me?" Frenchy whined. "You gonna keep me locked up?"

"You'll stay in for pulling that knife."

"I didn't know you was a lawman. The way you wear your coat, I didn't even see your badge."

"Hey! Me, too!" the red-headed cowhand shouted. "I didn't know you was sheriff. You didn't have no star on."

McQuade went to the iron-barred door. "Don't bother with the boxes." And to Billy, "Better stay around outside. See things are quiet."

The men began to leave, Seth Perrault looking again and again toward the cells. McQuade saw now that some of the hotel loungers had gathered just beyond the walk. When the three stepped outside, the loungers surged in on them to find out what had taken place. Seth began swearing, telling about the boxes angrily. Muttering and cursing broke out as the crowd crossed Union toward the hotel.

Mayor Appell asked, "Are you going to hold Gruber, too?"

"He interfered with an arrest, Mayor."

"Well." Appell paused, gazed around at the cells. "Word's getting around there were only harnesses and bridles in those boxes. If that driver pulled a knife on you, he should be locked up. But Gruber didn't commit any crime."

"That driver's a damned liar," McQuade said. He turned his back on Gruber and told Appell in a low voice what he'd found in the hotel and Frenchy's room.

Appell was shocked. "Oh, no," he muttered, stunned. He stared at English, who looked just as surprised. Appell shook his head. "No, George. They couldn't possibly know."

McQuade studied both men. "They couldn't know what?"

Appell exhaled slowly, and it was as though his rotund body had suddenly deflated. "Stillwell didn't tell you everything," he whispered. "He's holding a lot of money in the bank. Railroad money. Over a hundred thousand."

For a full minute McQuade didn't move. He looked out the window, and, while he gazed along the street, he could feel Appell and English studying his face. Finally, McQuade walked to where Gruber was sitting.

"You're through sticking your nose into the law in this town," he said.

Gruber wouldn't meet McQuade's stare. "I'm not the kind who can stand around and watch a man beaten."

"You'll stand around and watch anything I decide to do, Gruber. Either that or try facing me."

Gruber shrugged and glanced into the cell block. Then his eyes returned to McQuade. "You're wearin' the badge."

"That's right. Now get going."

McQuade stood silently beside the rolltop desk until Gruber reached the street. Then he walked back to Appell and English and said quietly, "I want to see Stillwell. Tell him to go to the bank. I'll meet him inside."

"This late?" Appell asked. "It'll be better if we go up to his house."

49

"I go up to Stillwell's house, everyone would realize something is going on. You tell Stillwell to make it look like he's just catching up on paper work."

"I know Henry Stillwell," Appell began. "He won't want to come—"

English cut in: "The marshal's right, John. This has got to be kept quiet. Stillwell's office is the best place." He nodded at McQuade. "You be at the bank in ten minutes, Marshal. Henry Stillwell will be there."

7

McQUADE MADE A QUICK ROUND of town before he went to the bank. Union had emptied after Seth Perrault and the others who'd carried the boxes into the jail had moved off, but, from the rumble of talk coming from the hotel saloon, McQuade knew where the townsmen had gone.

Near the bank porch he turned for one last survey of the long street. For a moment he glanced at the tracks of the Union Pacific, glistening in the moonlight. The tall redwood watertank beyond the depot stood like a motionless sentinel, guarding the rolling grass plain that stretched to the horizon. Only the rustle of the slight wind off the river sounded along the peaceful landscape, accenting the angry tones of the talk within the saloon. McQuade crossed the porch and knocked quietly.

He stepped inside as soon as George English opened the door. The room was long and L-shaped, with the north end beyond the two teller's windows built into an office. English halted at the office doorway to let McQuade enter first. Appell stood just inside the small room. He'd been talking to Stillwell, who was sitting at a wide mahogany desk, directly beneath a framed picture of President Chester A. Arthur.

Stillwell said irritably, "You've been here less than five hours, McQuade, and you're already giving everybody orders. I don't mind telling you I don't like it."

"Why didn't you tell me about the railroad money you're handling, Mr. Stillwell?"

"That's bank business. It has nothing to do with you."

McQuade's face remained easy. He took two steps closer to the desk and stood motionless while he looked down at Stillwell.

"How about the money, Mr. Stillwell?"

The banker leaned forward in his chair. "Appell was

wrong. The money won't get here until seven-thirty Saturday morning. It's all been planned so there'll be no danger."

"How much is coming?"

"One hundred and ten thousand."

"All in cash?"

Stillwell nodded. "This isn't the first time we've had money come through Farmington. We've handled two other shipments this large for the railroad." He smiled and rubbed his whiskered chin casually, satisfied he'd made his point. "We've never had so much as a threat of a robbery."

"You've got a threat now. You've still got time to wire Omaha and have that money held back."

Stillwell shook his head. "A great deal depends on our handling that money safely. It's more than just the money to us."

"That safety is gone," said McQuade. "Didn't the mayor tell you about the rifle and the bullets I found?"

"Voci's dead, McQuade. The fact you found bullets in that wagon-driver's room doesn't prove any threat to this bank. The three of us were just talking about that. We all go hunting. We keep cartridges in our homes. We certainly don't keep them as a threat to anyone or anything in Farmington."

Standing, Stillwell pulled the desk's middle drawer open and took out a large map of Nebraska. The spur line that ran south from Farmington had been inked in all the way to Kansas.

"This is the reason we're having the big time Saturday," he explained bluntly. "The railroad people are considering the erection of granaries here as soon as they finish the spur line. What do you think they'd do if we wired and told them this town is too dangerous even to have them ship their payroll through?"

"All right, Mr. Stillwell. Let the money come in. But there's no reason why the Wild West Show can't be canceled."

"No, we can't cancel that. It's up to us to prove to the railroad authorities we're the center of everything between Omaha and Ogallala. They'll see how many farmers we have in the county once we get them all into town. But those farmers wouldn't come in together unless we gave them an attraction. That attraction is Carson's show for their kids."

McQuade glanced at Appell and English. "You still go along with this?"

52

"We've done it before, Marshal," English remarked. "Even with half the town knowing about the money shipments, there has never been trouble."

"Do people here know about Saturday's shipment?"

"Only us three, and my tellers," Stillwell answered quickly. "And the railroad people."

"Which means anybody from here to Omaha could know," said McQuade.

Appell spoke up suddenly. "It's our big chance, Marshal. We can grow bigger than Omaha. We can become the most important farm center in the state." With a slight gesture at Stillwell, he continued, "Henry will only have the money until a train comes from the railroad camp. He has the guards all set up. There's really no danger."

"Seven or eight men will bring in the money," said Stillwell. "And there'll be three of us inside the bank."

"I still don't think it's worth the chance," McQuade stated.

"It doesn't matter what you think," Stillwell told him sharply. "We had this planned before you came into town and began kill—" He caught himself, knowing from McQuade's face he'd made a mistake. Feeling the blood drain from his own cheeks, he went on flatly, "No trouble has been connected to this bank. I'm not changing any plans simply because of what you think can happen."

Silence descended upon the small office. Mayor Appell stared down at the map, refusing to meet McQuade's eyes. English waited for McQuade to answer, but his gaze was on Stillwell. The banker straightened behind his desk and drew a deep breath, his face red and sweating.

McQuade swore to himself. He knew the greed and stupidity he faced could never be overruled by talk of the women and children who would've been out on Union under the weapons Voci and Frenchy had ready and waiting. Stillwell's argument would stand even if Voci wasn't dead, or if Frenchy wasn't locked up inside the jail.

"Okay," he said. "It's your bank, Mr. Stillwell." He gave the others a final glance, turned on his heel and walked from the office.

Appell remained quiet until he heard the outside door close. "What did he mean by that?" he said. "You don't think he's getting through?"

"I doubt that," said English.

"Well, I've got to know," Appell told them. He started for the door.

English took his arm and held him back. "I'll talk to him, John." Then, as soon as Appell stopped, English left the office.

English paused beyond the doorway to look up and down Union. Eight men, Tom Gruber among them, stood talking on the hotel porch. McQuade was halfway across the street, his tall form clearly visible in the floodlight glare of the moon. English stepped off the walk to follow. He once again pictured these few blocks as they'd be Saturday, the walks crowded right up to the porches, the street filled with the Wild West Show. It was still a foolproof plan, but there could be no slip-ups, not even minor ones.

Yes, it would work all right. He wouldn't be connected to anything. The only one who knew the newspaper was close to failing was Stillwell, and he'd be silenced in the holdup. It had all been settled in his agreement with Jake Clinton, even his talking the council into hiring McQuade.

Ahead, McQuade had heard English's footsteps. He'd halted, and as he turned he stepped into the shadows, keeping his back to the low wall of the feed storage shed.

English reached him, said, "I was looking for you, Marshal. We weren't certain what you intend to do."

"Not much I can do, Mr. English."

"You don't understand how we feel about Farmington." English glanced along Union. The moon gave a certain beauty to the town, illuminating the dusty land with a silvery light, and the same soft light reflected with a warm glow from the rooftops. "We've put every cent we have into our town. We're depending on it for our families."

"Then consider your families. Waiting until Monday for the shipment won't ruin your deal with the railroad."

"The railroad pays its crews on Saturday. And they're buying land south of here."

English, taking advantage of McQuade's silence, added, "You can see why Henry Stillwell couldn't ask that the shipment be held up until Monday."

"I see, Mr. English," said McQuade tiredly. He made no further comment, and English turned and started down Union. English had walked ten feet before he heard McQuade's step continue along the walk.

English, keeping to the center of the street, slowed his

54

pace while he walked past the men on the hotel porch. When he saw Gruber look his way, English nodded slightly, then continued on as though he hadn't noticed Gruber's questioning expression.

English went inside his newspaper office, but he didn't stop and light the lamp. He crossed the room and stepped out the rear door, then made his way through the thick blackness to the rear of the adjoining block. He'd reached the back of the hotel when he heard footsteps shuffle on the dry sand somewhere in the darkness ahead.

In another half minute his vision separated the shadows, identifying the man who was approaching from his walk. English pressed his body against the clapboards of the building and said in a low voice, "Gruber."

Gruber's bulky form halted and came toward English. "Mr. English, I don't—"

"Hold it down. Keep your voice down."

Gruber stopped. "I didn't know what you meant out there. I thought you wanted me to come around the paper office." He stood within a foot of English, near enough for the newspaperman's tall form to assume a definite shape. He wasn't sure of English's expression, but he knew his silence could be a mask to his quick anger.

After half a minute of quiet, English was sure neither of them had been followed. "Get your horse and lead him around to the depot. After, come into my office."

Gruber's heavy shoulders stiffened. He asked quickly, "You don't want me to ride anywhere tonight, Mr. English?"

"I'll do the riding. You'll be nice and safe inside, making it look like I'm in there working. Now, go ahead. Get the horse."

Opposite the marshal's office, Dan McQuade halted to look down the jail alleyway. The yard out back was dark and still, and there wasn't a light on in the house. McQuade sighed dejectedly. He'd hoped Ann would be up after he'd finished his rounds. Now he'd have no chance to talk to her until morning.

He continued along the walk toward the hotel. The men who'd been grouped on the porch had gone inside the saloon when they'd noticed his approach. McQuade could see them standing just beyond the batwings. He sensed their tension, felt it as one could feel the straining of a wire drawn too

55

tight. He glanced their way, and the watchful faces stared back.

The antagonism on these faces was clear, much simpler to read than the expressions he'd studied inside the bank. All during the round, McQuade had thought of what Stillwell and the others had said. He'd mulled over every word of the conversation, had judged every expression. He couldn't recall the slightest facial change that might have hinted that English or Appell suspected a bank robbery any more than the banker.

McQuade forgot the men in the saloon once he was by the batwings. He was passing the hotel lobby when he caught a movement just inside the doorway. His hand snapped back, down to his Colt.

"I've been waitin' to see you, Marshal."

The quick words came from the elderly clerk standing with his body against the doorjamb. McQuade let his hand drop all the way.

"You're stickin' your neck out, Marshal," Millett said. "All alone in the street like that."

"Didn't Ben Ford make his rounds like this?"

"Yes. But not when half the town—" He stopped as a man came down the staircase carrying a suitcase.

The man was well-dressed, clearly a visiting drummer. He glanced Millett's way but didn't speak as he walked through the lobby and into the saloon.

"That's the second check-out I've had tonight," Millett said. "There was a lot of talk in the saloon after them boxes were opened in your office."

"Men are going to take sides, Mr. Millett."

The clerk shook his head. "This talk didn't start tonight. It's been going on since before you came. The people are scared, and they can't hide it."

McQuade thought about that. Both Voci and Frenchy hadn't hesitated to jump him, and in both cases his winning had made the people a little more worried and afraid. The talk Millett mentioned, the attacks with a six-gun and knife —all were part of the pressure someone was directing personally against him. Now, McQuade decided, it was time to do a little squeezing himself.

"Don't worry, Mr. Millett," he said shortly. "You just keep those rooms ready. You'll have those people checking back in here soon."

8

THE NIGHT HAD PASSED SLOWLY for Jessup. He hadn't
slept at all, having forced himself to stay awake. The moon,
so brilliant during the early evening, still hung well clear of
the horizon, the way it shone gray-white on the prairie
giving him absolutely no cover. Now, catching some sound
out on the flat, he listened intently. Suddenly he got up fast.
He stood stiffly, strained to listen.

The prairie wind rustled the branches of the nearby
cottonwoods. Behind Jessup, somewhere beyond the moonlit
river, the warbling call of a night bird sounded. From the
west he heard the distant unmistakable drum of hoofs, and
relief coursed through him. Rubbing his bristled jaw and the
side of his face, he waited.

Fifteen minutes later he could make out the cattle. Close
to fifty head, he judged, from the size of the herd. A rider
pulled out in front of the cows when they were still a
quarter-mile away. Even in the dim light Jessup could
recognize Jake Clinton from the way he sat his saddle.

Jessup left the campfire and walked to the grass that
edged the river. He raised one hand in a wave, but Clinton
didn't wave back. Clinton swung his tall, husky body out of
the saddle, his movements quick and sure, his stubbled face
stony as he gave the fire and cottonwoods a long, searching
look. His tobacco-stained mouth cracked in a smile, but
there was no smile in his hard eyes.

"You and French decide to change places?" he asked.

"No," Jessup answered. While he told what had happened, he studied Clinton carefully, trying to judge how he
took the news. Clinton simply nodded and gazed around at
the cattle and riders. Jessup added, "Frenchy was supposed
to be back by now. I'm not sure he got to his gun."

"I know you're not sure," Jake Clinton said. "You're not
sure 'bout anythin' except that you ran the minute McQuade
told you to git."

57

Jessup flushed. "He would've locked me up if I tried staying. I figured I should get out here so you wouldn't try takin' them cows in." He paused, seeing how Clinton's face had tightened along the line of his jaw. "Look, Jake. We don't have to hit that bank. One of them trains might be easier."

"Both those trains'll be covered too damned good," Clinton said coldly. "We go in like we planned. We'll get inside the bank whether McQuade knows or not."

He spat a mouthful of tobacco juice and glanced beyond the cottonwoods to the river, where the other three riders had swung the steers. Jessup looked over, too. Cal Yates had stayed with the herd, and Dingo and Ed Clinton were walking their mounts toward the fire.

Dingo Clinton, a squat, thick-bodied man with a full black beard, held a lariat in his right hand. He tapped the rope slowly into the palm of his left as he talked to his brother Ed. He was swearing, but he kept his voice low and calm.

"What in hell is it now?" Jake Clinton said when they reached him. "I'm gettin' tired of this, Dingo."

Dingo cursed. "This fool kid. I don't get him. First he begs his way in on this, and soon as he's in he tries headin' everything. Now he don't want to tend the cattle and horses."

"Won't be no tendin' them cows," Jake Clinton told him. "McQuade started marshalin' in Farmington yesterday. He knows too many of us to try blockin' the street with the cattle."

"What do we do?" Ed Clinton rasped. "Change everythin' because McQuade's there? I thought we come here to get McQuade."

"We'll get him." Jake glared at his young cousin, looking him over from head to foot. Ed, a stringy, thin-chested man of twenty, with the sharp Clinton nose and square chin, was wearing a double gun-rig similar to Jake's own. "You save your cracks for your brother. Don't go pushin' someone who'll knock you down."

"I don't go for changes just because McQuade got in early. He's like any man. He gets a bullet in the gut, he don't last long."

"You dumb kid," Dingo said. "Don't go talkin' like a damn fool."

"It's worth a try," Ed said. "Why not?"

"McQuade's why not." Dingo swore and slapped the lariat against his leg. "Harry and Giles tried takin' him together. You saw how they ended up."

"They didn't do it like I'd—"

Jake Clinton grabbed his cousin's arm. "Quiet," he said, pointing to the horses. Two of the animals had lifted their heads, their ears cocked as they watched the brush to the east. "Tell Yates," he ordered, and Ed moved off toward the cattle.

Jake had both his six-guns out and ready. In that same instant, Dingo jerked his Spencer rifle from its saddle scabbard. Dingo pumped the weapon, and had it raised to his chest when a horse and rider broke from the willows twenty yards away.

It was George English. He rode to within a few feet of the men before he checked his mount.

"That's a good way to get killed," Jake Clinton said. He slid his twin Colts into their holsters.

"Not any more dangerous than all the talk I heard coming in here." English's eyes switched to Ed Clinton and Cal Yates, who'd appeared from the cluster of cottonwoods. "I'd have had you all stay at the soddy until Saturday if I thought you'd be foolish enough to shoot off your mouths like that."

"You would have had us, English?" said Jake Clinton.

Tense quiet stretched out as English swung down from the saddle and stepped forward. This put him in the center of a triangle, with Jake Clinton standing before him, Dingo on his left and Ed and Yates on the right. A faint sense of warning stirred in English. Holding his body calm, he raised his voice so it was louder, controlled.

"McQuade's got Frenchy in jail. There are some changes we should make, and battling among ourselves isn't going to help."

"Your changes have already cost me two men," said Jake Clinton. "The plan we got is good enough. Just as long as we get someone into the hotel."

"Not with the way McQuade's feeling around town. He'll have to be taken care of right away."

Ed Clinton said, "Hell, that would be easy enough. I could handle him myself."

"What's this you're talkin' up?" Dingo snapped. He grabbed his brother's arm and swung him around. "You wouldn't stand a chance facin' McQuade."

59

"I wouldn't have to face him. All's I got to do is stand in a doorway till McQuade walks past."

"You don't pull nothin' like that, kid. Get that straight."

English said, "Let him talk."

Dingo turned on English. "Listen, mister. You don't stick this kid's neck out. Get that clear." His eyes, switching to Jake Clinton, left no doubt about the person he felt was boss. "The kid don't go in, Jake."

English ignored him and questioned Ed. "You're willing to try?"

"Sure. I wouldn't have to be alone." Ed glanced at Yates, a stringy man dressed in a gray shirt and Levis. "McQuade don't know me or Cal. We could get him easy."

"It sounds good," English said. He surveyed Ed with cool speculation and liked what he saw. Ed was on edge, ready to show he could measure up. All he'd have to do was stand around and wait for McQuade to step out of the jail. English spoke to Jake Clinton. "I say they can do it."

"I don't know." Jake's black eyes frowned, his whiskered features set in a closed, unrevealing expression.

"I do," English said. "We do it like this or the whole thing is off."

"No, it won't be off," Jake said, correcting him. "We can kill McQuade and take that bank without you, English."

"We made a deal, Clinton." There was no pretense in English's voice or stare. "I was to get McQuade out of Arizona where you could get at him. You agreed to steal the railroad money. McQuade's in Farmington. You decide if you're going to hold up your end."

Jake Clinton smiled slightly, but it didn't relieve the closed expression on his face. He said to Ed, "Okay, you'll go in."

"Ed ain't goin'," warned Dingo. "He ain't, Jake."

Jake Clinton shifted his stance, stretching his legs and right arm while he moved. His expression had changed, making him seem almost sleepy. "I think it's a perfect setup, Dingo. Only Yates ain't goin' in. I am."

English shook his head. "McQuade knows you. You won't stand a chance."

"With these whiskers, I will. He won't get that close a look anyway. I go with Ed."

"I'm goin' with Yates," Ed protested. "I don't need no more'n him."

60

"I'm goin'," Jake Clinton said sharply. "That's the only way you get to go." He looked at Dingo. "What you say?"

Dingo stared at Jake, his hand frozen on the Spencer's stock. His eyes flicked to his brother and saw that Ed was waiting. Dingo licked his lips, his face intent. "Okay, Jake. No chances, though."

"There won't be."

Ed made a gesture of disgust. "Ahh!" he grunted angrily. He whirled on his boot heels and stalked to the place where he'd left his horse. Jake Clinton took a step after him.

"That cattle, Jake," said English. And when Clinton stopped, he said, "You'll still drive it in. We better leave one man here until Saturday. The rest should go back to the soddy, just in case any farmers begin to wonder why so many men are here."

Clinton nodded, spoke to Jessup. "You stay with the cows."

"Why me, Jake?" Jessup complained. "That was Ed's job."

"The way you ran from McQuade, I figured you'd want to be nice and safe, blockin' the road." He took the Spencer from Dingo's hand and held it out to Jessup. "Just make damned sure those cows are here to take in Saturday."

Without an answer, Jessup accepted the carbine. Then he turned and walked to the river, where the cattle were still watering.

The earliest rays of the sun brightened the rooftops along Farmington's business district before the yellowish-violet daylight settled lower to splash across the Nebraska flat, chasing the night shadows before it. The first trace of light filtering in through the window of the marshal's office woke Dan McQuade.

He swung his legs off the bunk he'd used as a bed and checked the sleeping prisoners in the other cells. As he stood, he took the makings from his shirt pocket. Expertly, he flaked out the tobacco, rolled a lean cigarette and lit it. He was motionless for a few seconds, his eyes on the wanted posters he'd tacked up last night and on the gunrack he'd spent an hour shifting to a spot midway between the two office doors.

He opened the front door and gazed along Union Street. Nothing moved in the complete quiet. Here and there lamplight showed in houses behind the business district. Thin columns of smoke rose from chimneys to indicate that breakfast was being started.

McQuade, exhaling a mouthful of smoke, relaxed in the peaceful silence. But, when his eyes moved to the area between the hotel and the blacksmith shop, he tightened inside. McQuade dropped the cigarette and ground it out on the walk. Turning, he walked through the office and out the back way.

There was a tin washbasin on the curb of the well. McQuade filled it and returned to the towel and razor on his desk. He had just finished his shave when Billy Ford came in.

"Morning," McQuade said.

The deputy eyed the posters and the new position of the gunrack. "Mornin'—goin' to be a hot one."

McQuade nodded and dropped the soggy towel into the basin. "I've set up a schedule for us. We'd better both be on days until after Carson's show leaves."

"Sure. I'll split tonight if you want. It's all quiet after nine or ten anyway."

"No. I'll stay in here over the weekend."

Billy rubbed a hand across his mouth. "My first round's usually before eight. I'll get started on it."

"I'll make it today," McQuade said. Taking his Stetson from the desk, he pressed in the torn crown. "You feed those two. And tell Frenchy I'm letting him go."

"Look," Billy demanded, straightening his shoulders. "If all I'm goin' to do is get them prisoners' meals, I'm—"

"You get their meals," McQuade told him. "After that, tell the hostler to get Frenchy's horse out of the livery."

Billy glowered. "I'm no waiter, Marshal."

"You're my deputy," said McQuade flatly. "Like any working deputy, you'll follow orders."

McQuade didn't wait for an answer. He picked up the wash basin and went into the yard. He was almost to the well when sharp words from the barn startled him.

"Get 'em up!"

McQuade had whirled to face the building with a breath-stopping twist of his body that swerved him to the left and shot his right hand down to his holster before he was fully aware it had been a boy's voice.

Stevie pushed open the barn door and stepped outside. He was grinning, holding an aimed .44. McQuade, letting out a long breath, started toward the boy.

"Bang!" Stevie said. "Bang! Bang!" Then, laughing, "That how you do it, Marsh'l? That how a lawman does it?"

"Something like that." He took the revolver from the boy's hand. It was an ancient Navy cap-and-ball Colt, minus a hammer. "Steve, I don't want you to do anything like that again. Don't you ever let me catch you pointing a gun at anyone."

"That's broke." Stevie was still grinning, but uncertainly now. "It don't take bullets. And the trigger's busted."

"It doesn't matter. Never point any kind of gun at anyone. Never. Who gave you it anyway?"

"I found it in Grandpa's room."

"You put it back there. You're too young to be handling a gun, even a broken gun."

"Aw, gee, Marsh'l. I was only foolin'." Near tears, he held the revolver in both hands, muzzle down. "Can't have any fun 'round here. Ain't nothin' to do 'round here." He turned and headed toward the barn.

"Steve," McQuade said.

The boy turned around, looking so unhappy McQuade had to smile at him. He walked to Stevie and put a hand on one small shoulder.

"There's a lot for you to do," he said, pointing at the horses in the two close stalls. "They look like they haven't been fed. You can get them what they need."

Steve sniffed. "Mommy does that. She don't want me near the horses."

"You won't have to go too near them. Just be careful to keep out in the aisle, that's all. I'll talk to your mother. Here, I'll take the gun inside."

"I'll be careful." Stevie held out the Colt. "Don't worry, Marsh'l."

"I won't worry."

"You're not mad at me, are you?"

"No. You remember about not pointing guns. Even when you're old enough to have a gun of your own, you remember."

"Okay," Stevie said, and he ran across the yard.

McQuade watched the boy sprint away, then turned to the house. Ann stood behind the screen door, looking at him. He wondered how long she'd been there, how much she'd heard. He stopped on the porch and held out the

63

revolver for her to take. "You better keep this where Steve can't get it," he said.

She hesitated uncertainly, gazing at the barn. "Stevie hasn't been close to horses much. He isn't used to them."

"Well, this is a good chance for it. Besides, it'll give the boy a little responsibility mornings before he goes to school."

She put her hand to her hair, still watching the barn. There was a moment of silence, and then she opened the door. "I made extra breakfast for you, Dan." She paused. "I thought—"

"Smells mighty good. Man'd be a fool to turn down ham and eggs that smell like that."

Ann smiled, but her expression was somewhat strained. The kitchen, large and high-ceilinged with white curtains and immaculate floor and furniture, was just as he remembered her home in Tombstone, nice-feeling and orderly. While she filled a plate at the stove, he pulled out the chair opposite the door and sat.

She set the plate in front of him. "I didn't mean to be so abrupt last night."

"You don't have to explain. No reason to."

She remained silent, and he started to eat. In the quiet she added some wood to the stove, shook the fire, turned the charred sticks and put her wash into a large pot of boiling water. McQuade ate slowly, without talking, yet he followed every movement she made.

Finally he said, "This is good, coming in for a meal like this. That's one of the things I missed after you left with the baby."

Ann didn't look around, but stirred the clothes, careful not to spill the steaming water. She covered the pot, then took the skillet and put it into the sink. He waited until she had begun the dishes, then said, "You didn't have to run like that."

She turned to face him. Her cheeks were flushed from the heat, but the look of strain was still apparent. "You let me know you'd never give up being a lawman. And you'd been so good to us, visiting every day, taking care of everything. I knew it was because you pitied us, Dan, but I'd started to feel close to you. Too close. I couldn't even allow myself to think of becoming a lawman's wife again."

"It wasn't pity. Not after the first couple months. I wouldn't've taken this job if I hadn't hoped there'd be a

64

chance for me with you and the boy." He looked directly into her face. "These last seven years, you've always been a part of my thoughts. You'll always be."

"Dan, there are other women."

McQuade took a deep breath and set the fork down on the table. "No, Ann. Not for me."

"There will be. There are women who can accept the life you have to live. I couldn't do it even before Steve was killed. I can't do it now. Those months I did stay in Tombstone, I watched you. It got so I was waiting for a gunfight every time you walked the street. I saw you lying face down in the street, bleeding . . " Her hand rose and gestured as though she meant to touch him, but it fell once more to her side.

"So you just picked up and left without telling me. Knowing I loved you, and that the boy needed a father. Like he needs one now."

"He'll have one now." She had glanced away from him toward the railroad. The shrill whistle of the morning express passing the town sounded clearly. Again she met his stare. "I'm sorry it had to be this way. But it really ended back in Tombstone, didn't it, Dan?"

"For you it did."

Ann didn't answer. He pushed back from the table, stood and hitched his gunbelt higher. His expression softened, relieved by a small, tentative smile. "I was going to check your horses."

Ann nodded, understanding in her eyes. He gazed around, saw that she had taken his Stetson and put it on a chair. He went to pick it up.

"That crown," she said. "I'll fix it. It'll only take a few minutes."

He pushed a finger through the jagged tear and nodded. "I'll make sure Steve knows how to handle the horses," he told her. Then he went outside.

Stopping at the barn doorway long enough to roll and light a cigarette, he looked around the yard as he blew out the match, his glances reading more into the place than he had yesterday. The barn was roomier than it seemed from the outside. There was work that needed to be done, too, little jobs a man usually does. Barely enough hay had been set out for the horses, and Steve was busy forking some down from the loft. Winter storms had loosened shingles, letting in the spring rain. Another good wind would rip

65

more off. A few would have to be replaced, and the rest nailed flat again.

McQuade moved inside and halted between the front stalls. The two horses watched him warily, shying away from the smell of the cigarette. The claybank mustang was the one he decided on. He was big, and had good lines that showed evidence of stamina and speed.

McQuade, stepping close to the claybank's stall, spoke quietly to the animal. The horse backed away from him, but after a minute's talk it was completely calm. McQuade smiled, dropped the cigarette and ground it out with his boot heel before he entered the stall. The claybank tossed his head, yet it was no longer frightened. McQuade stroked its neck and flanks.

Steve climbed down from the loft and began to carry the hay into the bin. His clear blue eyes sparkled, and he grinned.

"I like doin' this," he said.

"Good. You can feed them every morning before you go to school. So your mother won't have to do it."

"Yuh." The boy started past the horse.

"Careful," McQuade warned. "Never walk too close to a horse's rump. They don't kick often, but you never can be sure."

McQuade heard the swish of a dress beyond the door. He glanced around.

"Mom! Look, Mom. I'm feeding the horses!" Stevie let the hay drop, ran and grabbed his mother's arm. "Look, I got the hay down!"

"Hey," McQuade said. "The horse can't eat it out in the aisle."

Steve knelt and swept up an armful of hay. Ann smiled at her son, then looked seriously at McQuade. "Reno was Dad's horse. Are you going to try him?"

"Later. After I make the morning round."

She nodded, the serious expression remaining while she held out his hat for him to take. "This will last until you get a chance to buy a new one."

"Thanks, Ann." McQuade glanced at the boy. "Not too close now, Steve. Just put it where he can get at it. Here, I'll show you."

Ann watched her son and McQuade for a minute, then left the barn and returned to the kitchen to busy herself with the dishes. The emotion she'd felt when she'd left Arizona

66

was strong again, somehow, seeing McQuade with Stevie, watching how he handled the boy. Regrets and remorseful thoughts had come to her from time to time, but, as the years had slipped past, her life taken up by Stevie and her teaching, she'd found she could put the wishful thoughts about Dan McQuade out of her mind.

She shook her head. What was wrong with her? She was no young bride now, but a grown woman, a woman who'd made her own life for seven long years. Regrets and wishful thoughts were allowable, yet they shouldn't remain with her. She'd been purposely cold and matter-of-fact with Dan, and she'd convinced him there was nothing left for them.

She moved to the stove and stirred the wash. She'd noticed how Dan had picked the chair that faced the door. He couldn't relax or feel really safe, not even in her kitchen. No—the calm, peaceful life, the life George English represented, was what she wanted. George had done so much in Farmington, and he'd do bigger, better things in Omaha. As his wife she could help him.

Once more she shook her head. It wasn't George who bothered her. It was Dan McQuade. He seemed so tired, his face so worn, with eyes that searched for understanding.

Through the window she saw Dan appear from the barn and cross the yard toward the alleyway to Union Street. She thought of her Stevie's grin, his excitement in the barn, and she was tempted to call out. Her pulse beat strongly in her breast, but she didn't move. Her future with George English was assured; with Dan there would be only more worry and anxiety and pain.

Ann leaned closer to the window and watched McQuade until he vanished between the buildings. "Oh, Dan Dan," she whispered.

9

To THE EAST THE SUN was higher above the horizon, burning away the last of the night chill. Long shadows stretched across the dusty width of Union. A few townspeople were already out along the walks, getting their shopping done early. Three bonneted housewives, who were standing in front of the general store watching Appell's gangling young clerk lower the gray- and white-striped awning, made a visible effort to keep to themselves as McQuade walked past.

McQuade, crossing back toward the jail, was aware of this, just as he felt the silent, cautious glances of the others he'd met during his round of the town. There was more open hostility in the stares today, more controlled worry than he'd seen yesterday.

"Marshal! Say, Marshal!"

The hail halted McQuade before he had stepped onto the boardwalk of the marshal's office. He turned. Mayor Appell had just come out of the restaurant. His round, serious face studied McQuade's as he hurried along the walk.

"Billy Ford got some meals from inside," he said, panting from his run. "And he told them to get Frenchy's horse ready at the livery."

"That's right, Mayor. I'm letting both of those cowhands out by the time Carson's show's over."

Appell, wiping one pudgy hand across his mouth, asked in a quieter voice, "Then you don't think there's any danger from them at the bank?"

"No, Mayor. I haven't changed my mind about that." The distant sounds of pounding and sawing made McQuade glance toward lower Union. Carpenters had started work on some lumber there. A few of the town men had grouped around to watch what they were constructing.

"That a bandstand they're building?" McQuade asked.

"It's a platform for the show tomorrow. It'll be used by the council members and their families."

"The show's going to be put on in the street?"

Appell nodded. "Union is wide enough. We thought it would be easier that way. There's no danger. The walks will be roped off."

McQuade was quiet for a few moments as he surveyed the length of the street. The platform would go almost clear across and close off the east end. With the size of the expected crowd, the walks would be jammed, blocking every way out of town but upper Union.

McQuade said, "If I need extra deputies, how about you?"

The mayor became fidgity, looked at the platform. "I'd rather not, Marshal. I've got a wife and two children."

"They'll be in the audience tomorrow."

"I want to be near them. It's my duty as—"

"It's the duty of every citizen to see the law is backed," said McQuade flatly.

Appell's fat face reddened. "My own family comes first. You can understand that." He avoided McQuade's eyes. "We thought it would be even safer with our kids on a platform."

"For them, it might be," McQuade said. He stepped up and crossed the walk. A foot inside the threshold he stopped. There would be a parade, as there always was in these wild west shows. It would have to come down from the siding, and the only street that could serve as an exit was Depot. The windows in the hotel and the blacksmith's overlooked every inch that would be used tomorrow. McQuade's face was wooden, his mouth tightened in concentration.

Billy Ford came out of the cell block. "They're fed," he said. "I told Frenchy you're lettin' him out."

Nodding, McQuade said, "Take the dishes over to the restaurant. Then come right back."

"Hell, the Dutchman can come after these dishes."

"You take them back," McQuade said. "The one thing we have to do is make things look normal till after Frenchy rides out." He waited for Billy to answer. When the deputy did not speak, McQuade went past him into the cell block.

The red-headed cowhand stood with his face close to the vertical bars. "How come he gets out and I don't?" he called. "I didn't pull no knife on you."

"You'll get out in due time," McQuade told him. He stopped at Frenchy's cell and unlocked the door. The huge man did not speak, and nothing could be learned from his dark features as he waited for McQuade to talk.

"Ride out of town and stay out," McQuade ordered. "Is that clear?"

"What 'bout my knife?"

"I'm keeping that. I see you in this town again, there'll be two charges against you."

Frenchy nodded, touched the bandage over his left ear. "I don't want no more trouble."

"All right. Get going."

Frenchy started past him. From the other cell the red-head whined, "Hey, what 'bout me? I wanta look for a job with Carson."

"I'll let you talk to Carson," McQuade said. "You stay right there, you won't get into any trouble before his show comes."

The cowhand stared at Frenchy, going through the office, and at McQuade. He looked angry, as though he meant to say more, but without a word he walked to his bunk and sat down.

McQuade closed both doors to the cell block. He waited at the window until Frenchy rode out of the blacksmith's on his horse. Then McQuade crossed the office and took a Winchester .73 from the gun rack.

He had the rifle loaded by the time Billy Ford returned to the office. McQuade motioned toward the yard and said, "Saddle your father's claybank. Keep him inside till Frenchy's clear of town."

"What?" Billy's voice was high. "I'm a deputy, not—"

"You saddle that horse, mister. Fast, or you'll be an ex-deputy."

Billy glared at McQuade and started around the desk. He was silent as he watched McQuade draw his Colt to check its load. "I'll do it," Billy said gruffly. "But there's one thing I want you to know."

McQuade glanced up. "I'm listening."

"You can give me every dirty job you've got. But you can't make me quit. You get that clear."

"Good," McQuade said. "Because as soon as Carson's show leaves town, you'll get to work in the barn. You can at least get that roof fixed before I take over the house."

Billy stood flat-footed. He took a deep breath, muttered a curse and walked into the yard.

McQuade rotated the Colt's drum before he slid the weapon into the holster again. He stepped to the front door and saw that Frenchy had cut into Depot Street from lower Union, heading north. McQuade smiled. It was just what he'd expected the huge man to do.

Billy had finished with the cinch when McQuade reached the barn. McQuade stepped up beside him and put the Winchester into the boot.

"Go down by the station," he said. "See what direction Frenchy finally heads."

The deputy swung around. His face was still bitter as he walked past the barn. McQuade patted the claybank's neck and spoke to it in a low voice before he mounted.

He kneed the horse ahead and stopped just inside the doorway. He heard the sound of running feet, then saw little Stevie Heath come out of the alleyway beside the jail. The boy ran straight to the barn.

"Marsh'l! That cowboy you fought's outta jail, Marsh'l!" he blurted. "I saw him ride by the schoolyard!"

"I know, Steve. I let him out."

The house back door opened, and Ann carried a basket of clothes onto the porch. Seeing McQuade and her son, she set the basket under the clothesline and crossed to the doorway.

"Stevie, I thought you'd gone to school."

"I saw that cowboy the marsh'l fought ridin' outa town. I had to tell him, Mom."

"You get back. Hurry. The bell will ring in a few minutes."

She watched the boy run off, then studied McQuade. "You still suspect that man. You're going to follow him."

McQuade nodded. He pulled the claybank to the right so he could look directly into her eyes, sitting so close to her they both felt the sudden tension. She started to speak, but then Billy appeared at the corner of the barn.

"Frenchy turned west,' he said. "He's headin' toward the river."

Nodding again, McQuade kneed the horse forward.

"Dan—" Ann said. And when he glanced around, she added, "Be careful."

"I will, Ann."

71

She stood in the doorway until McQuade turned into the alleyway, holding the claybank in close to the barn.

"What you doin', Ann?" Billy said, his voice crisp. "Comin' out here like this?"

"Why shouldn't I?"

"Oh, come on." Her brother gestured at the barn with an irritated jerk of his chin. "You're gettin' too friendly with McQuade. And you know it."

She shook her head. "Don't worry, Billy. That's all there is to it." Stressing the last few words, she walked toward the clothesline.

Billy didn't move for a few seconds as he took in her answer. He started after her, but then stopped. "Don't let it be any more than that," he called. "I mean it, Ann."

10

GEORGE ENGLISH HAD WAITED PATIENTLY for Jake and Ed Clinton to appear. The night's chill had burned off into a hot, sultry day, and English found himself slowly growing impatient. He'd watched for McQuade, too, but hadn't seen him since he'd made his round just before eight. English hadn't stepped out of his office once all morning. He couldn't take any chance of being in the street when the gunfire started. That way there wouldn't be even the remotest possibility of anyone connecting him to what happened, now or later.

Somewhere in the rooms on the second floor, a clock struck the hour. English looked up from his desk and counted. "Ten," he muttered. "What's taking them so long?"

English stood and walked to the window. He scowled when he thought of the Clintons. Actually it had been a mistake to let Jake bring his two cousins with him. He'd needed Jake, but he hadn't thought of the possibility of the Clinton family lining up against him. He wasn't as certain as before that the Clintons would be easy to handle if anything went wrong.

English suddenly straightened and stepped back from the window. He'd caught sight of the two riders crossing the railroad tracks beyond the depot.

He watched Jake and Ed Clinton pull their horses left to circle around and come in the town's back way.

English did not return to his work immediately after the Clintons had disappeared behind the buildings. For a fraction of a minute his gaze rested on the bank. Twenty-four hours from now there would be more than a hundred thousand dollars taken from its safe. Fifty thousand would be in his own pocket within a week. No one could stop that once McQuade was dead.

Jake Clinton's hard eyes were cautious, his tall body

73

slightly hunched as he pulled his pinto in behind the hotel. He'd studied each alleyway, each door at the rear of the buildings, anything that moved, always ready in case McQuade had seen him and Ed cut around back. They had the element of surprise over McQuade, and Jake Clinton meant to keep it.

"McQuade shows, wait'll I move," he muttered to his cousin while they dismounted. "I'll do the talkin' in here."

Ed nodded, whipped a halter knot around the worn rail. He fell in behind Jake and followed him through the hotel's rear entrance.

Millett, sitting behind the registration desk, stood when he observed the two armed men step into the lobby. Eyes flicking from them to the street, he spoke before they reached him.

"Better check them guns, gents. The marshal's arrestin' anyone who breaks the no-gun law."

Jake Clinton said, "We want rooms."

"Sorry, they're all taken. Listen, you'd better let me check them guns."

"That marshal got a room here?" Jake swung the ledger around and ran a long finger down the list of names. "Yeah, here he is." His cold eyes bore into the old clerk's. "We'll take McQuade's room."

Millett grinned, as though something funny had been said, but his mouth closed when Jake began signing the ledger. Millett shifted uncomfortably. "Listen, a joke's a joke, but don't make any trouble for me. Please."

"This is no joke," Ed said.

The clerk turned the ledger, his red-veined face intent on the page. He gulped, drew away from the desk. "I'm sorry, Mr. Clinton. Really sorry."

"Get that room cleaned out," Jake snapped. Turning, he led the way through the lobby to the screen door. The street was quiet, with townspeople going about their business. He saw no sign of McQuade, and from where he stood the marshal's office looked empty.

"I'll take my horse 'round back of the jail," he told Ed. "You wait five minutes and come across." Suddenly, at a noise behind him, he whirled and scanned the lobby. "Hey, you!"

Millett, halfway to the saloon, halted at the order. He turned his small face to the saloon doorway, seeking a way of escape.

Jake walked back toward Millett. "Where you goin'?" He glowered, but Ed seemed amused.

The clerk swallowed. "Just into the saloon, Mr. Clinton. Honest."

"You were goin' t' tell McQuade," Jake said. He waved at his cousin. "You wanted some fun. Teach him."

Ed grinned and moved forward. Millett edged away, his cheeks pale with fear. One of Ed's hands caught him and swung him around. Millett let out a high-pitched shriek as Ed's fist smashed into his face and blood spurted from his nose. Ed's second blow to the stomach doubled him over, and Millett grunted and crumpled to the floor.

Jake stood over the prostrate old man. "Get up. Up." He grabbed Millett's shoulder and jerked him to his feet. "Get behind that desk and keep shut."

"I will. Right now. I will."

Jake held the small, veined face close to his own. "One of us'll be inside this door. You tell no one we're here." He shoved Millett into the desk so hard the old man went sprawling.

"Get up," Ed said.

Millett pushed himself up fast, went around behind the desk and stayed there.

"They'll know who we are," Jake said to Ed. "I'll get goin' now."

Ann Heath had thought about McQuade all morning. Billy's words in the yard had made her realize she'd allowed herself to go too close to Dan, to feel near to him again. She shook her head quickly as she left the ironing board and crossed the kitchen to exchange the iron she had been using for a heated one. She put down the cool iron, took the other and tested it with a finger. Dan loved her, had never let himself forget her. And he needed a woman, maybe even more than most men need one.

She knew she'd played the coward all along. For her there had been no other way. But there had always been a presence of deep loss in her mind, too. If she had stayed, to help him, to face whatever he faced, the dangers ... If she thought she could stand beside him now ...

She looked out the window, along the side of the barn where McQuade had ridden off. The sun was halfway up the sky, with only a few cottony clouds dotting the immense stretch of blue. It would be a driving heat on the prairie today.

A man had rounded the far corner of the barn, a whiskered, tall man who walked too carefully to be merely cutting through to the street. Ann set the iron back on the stove and went out on the porch.

The man was closer now, and she saw he was wearing two guns and holding one of the revolvers in his left hand. Ann felt herself turn sick, but she didn't move. The man watched her as he slid around to the front of the barn. Once in the clear, he broke into a run for the rear door of the marshal's office.

He was inside only a few seconds before he reappeared. He walked directly to the porch.

"Where's McQuade?" Jake Clinton asked.

Ann managed to keep her voice strong. "The new marshal? He'd be around town."

His deep black eyes didn't change. "You his woman?"

"No. My brother is the deputy. He's around town, too."

Jake studied her thoughtfully. A vagrant wind stirred the kitchen curtains and flapped them and then ceased. Ed Clinton appeared from the office doorway. He held both of his six-guns and kept them ready as he crossed the yard.

"McQuade ain't in there," he told Jake. "That door to the cell block's locked from the office side. We can get—"

"We do nothin' till we get McQuade. He's somewhere 'round town."

" 'Kay. We'll go together," Ed said, his voice shaded with impatience. "He'll be easy enough to find."

Jake shook his head. "We'll let him walk into it." He holstered his Colt, eyed Ann and smiled at his cousin. "You wait in the hotel till he goes into the office. I'll wait here."

Ed nodded, "Soon as he's goin' inside, I'll get him."

"No, don't try that. Wait 'til I get a clear shot, too. He's too much for you alone."

Ed, mumbling a curse, dropped his weapons into their holsters. "Maybe he's not that tough."

Jake's whiskered face tightened. "Don't try it, kid."

Ed's eyes ran over Ann, and he nodded. "Like you say," he grunted, and crossed toward the alleyway.

Dan McQuade had kept to the cottonwood-dotted willow thickets on the north bank of the Platte for the last hour. Frenchy was now a small dark figure far ahead, lost from view most of the time in the rolling swells of endless grass and sky.

McQuade had passed close to thirty farms already, half a dozen of them large places with wooden buildings, the rest little more than soddies dug into ridge slopes with willow-pole roofs and doorways. They held good promise, though, for the land this side of the river had rich topsoil for grazing, hay and crops. With the granaries Stillwell and Appell had spoken of, they'd all be thriving farms within three to five years.

Stillwell and Appell hadn't overestimated their future, McQuade well realized. If anything, they'd barely scratched the surface of possibilities in the area.

McQuade reined in quickly behind the cover of the willows. Frenchy had pulled up, and was sitting looking back along the trail. McQuade couldn't see what was beyond the trees, but he could hear the bawling of cattle coming from that direction.

Instantly he moved the claybank deeper into the willows. The sound of the cattle reached him again, mixed noises with that particular tone that told him the cows weren't being driven. Frenchy, still motionless, kept staring along his backtrail. After another half-minute, he angled his black toward the woods.

McQuade sat perfectly still, forgetful of the humming mosquitoes that deluged him, straining his eyes against the sun's glare to see how many men were ahead waiting for Frenchy.

He held back until Frenchy reached the edge of the willows; then he kneed the claybank forward slowly.

Five hundred yards ahead, the cattle were making too much noise for Jessup. He'd never noticed before how much of a racket their bawling made, mainly because every other time he'd driven herd he'd had other punchers with him. When he'd first spotted a rider coming along the flat a few minutes ago, he'd felt cold fear run all through his body. But now, seeing it was Frenchy, he exhaled his drawn breath and let himself relax.

Jessup started out of the cottonwoods. He had raised one hand to wave, and was just about to yell. Then he saw the second rider, who was following a good mile behind Frenchy.

For one frozen instant Jessup let his wild fear stop him where he stood. Then, by sheer reaction, he dropped and rolled behind a thick tree trunk. One swift grab brought Dingo Clinton's Spencer rifle into his hands.

Frenchy jerked his bandana over his mouth, took off his sombrero and battled at mosquitoes as his horse broke through the thicket. He didn't notice Jessup until he was almost on top of him. Jessup was lying flat, sprawled out behind the thick trunk of the middle cottonwood. He waved one hand wildly at Frenchy.

"Keep going," Jessup called in a low voice. "Don't turn your head. You're bein' tailed."

"What—who, McQuade?"

"Can't tell yet. Keep ridin'." He raised the barrel of the Spencer and motioned with it to the flat. "He'll come after you. I'll get him."

"Gimme my gun. I'll get him."

"No. No, keep ridin'. I'll catch up."

Frenchy swore, but he reined the black to the right so he'd be in clear view of whoever was following him.

McQuade held down his mount when he saw Frenchy was keeping to the edge of the timber, not going in as he'd believed. He could see the cattle, about fifty head, crowded into a small, meadowlike stretch that ran to the river.

He decided to let Frenchy get his mile lead back and, slowing the claybank even more, rode like that for three minutes.

The shot came as a complete surprise. The sharp crash of a rifle came instantaneously with a sound like a hand slapping hard on the neck of the claybank. A tuft of mane hairs flew. The animal whinnied in pain, gave a jerk of its head convulsively and began to go down.

McQuade made a desperate effort to draw his booted rifle, but the horse fell straight forward, taking the weapon out of McQuade's reach.

McQuade dove from the saddle. Earth smashed his forehead, gravel tearing the flesh. He rolled fast to the left and the cover of the low-growing brush.

A second shot blasted the air and echoed into the river and the timber along the flat. Screams went up from the cattle. They started their fear-stricken run, stampeding by instinct away from the gunfire.

Colt in hand, McQuade lay prone, searching in the direction of the bushwhacker, the five cottonwoods clustered ahead about a hundred yards. The claybank's hoofs pounded the ground as the wounded animal kicked to right itself.

Another bullet came from the cottonwoods. A small

crater of dirt mushroomed a foot from McQuade's right shoulder. McQuade leveled the .44, fired once and made three rolls to the left, deeper into the tangled brush.

The claybank was up, terrified, charging out of the willows toward the flat. Two quick shots sounded, and both bullets smacked loudly into the horse. The animal bellowed in pain, stumbled and crashed to earth again.

McQuade swore and pushed himself up onto one knee. He fired once, and again. Then, crouching, he made a zigzagging dash to close in on the bushwhacker.

Another rifle shot exploded, the steel slug zinging into the dust inches from McQuade's leg. McQuade had covered half the distance to the cottonwoods now. Surer this time, he aimed carefully and put two bullets in low.

Dead silence fell.

McQuade ran forward, fired another low bullet and heard it whack the bottom of a tree trunk.

A confused scrambling sounded ahead and, immediately after, the noise of a horse crashing through the brush.

Ten seconds later McQuade reached the cottonwoods, gun ready. He halted once he saw the empty carbine shells behind the largest tree trunk.

He stood there and reloaded his Colt, listening for any sound. Hearing none, he walked to where the claybank lay.

One bullet had gone through the horse's neck high up. The last two had hit squarely in the chest. It had been a quick death, but McQuade cursed himself for not being able to save the animal.

He drew the Winchester from its boot and leaned it against a tree. Then he took the saddle and bridle off the head horse and hid them in the brush.

He stared for another few seconds at the scattered cattle, trying to figure out just why the bushwhacker had waited here with so many cows. Finally he picked up the Winchester and started the long walk back to Farmington.

Ann had waited in the hot kitchen for the last two hours, watching the whiskered man keep his lookout for McQuade. He'd gone down to the far end of the barn three times. He'd stayed there ten minutes the first time, close to fifteen the second. He'd been there three minutes this third time.

Ann lifted the clothes basket and went outside to the line. She busied herself with taking down the wash at the house end, and worked slowly to a spot where she'd be out of the gunman's view in front of the barn. But her brother Billy threatened to spoil her plans.

He looked out the office doorway suddenly and called to her, "How about dinner, Ann?"

She didn't stop unpinning the clothes. She folded a dish-towel and laid it in the basket. Casually, she shook her head with exasperation and spoke irritatedly.

"Go over to the restaurant, Billy. I'll be another hour with all these things to iron."

Billy moved out onto the steps and studied her quizzical-ly. "What about Stevie? He'll be out of school in a few minutes."

"I'm just giving him cereal. You go ahead, Billy. I've got packing to do after."

Her brother stood in the doorway, watching her for another long minute before he turned inside.

She wondered if the bearded gunman had heard what had been said. There was no way she could tell. He'd neither changed position nor said anything. He didn't seem to be paying attention to her, but let her continue to work out of his sight unchallenged.

Once she was sure she couldn't be seen, Ann dropped the pillowcase she'd taken off the line and ran for the barn. She didn't stop until she reached Billy's saddle. Carefully, as noiselessly as possible, she lifted it and lugged it into the bay's stall. She hadn't even gotten to the cinch when she heard loud footsteps behind her.

"What in hell you tryin'?"

Ann stood dumfounded. She didn't scream; she couldn't. She stood straight as Jake Clinton closed in on her.

"Tryin' to get out, were you?" Cursing, he swung with his open right hand. The blow slammed furiously across her face, knocking her against the side of the stall. Starting to taste her own blood, she put her fingers up to stop the bleeding.

"Get back inside. Go 'head, get goin'!" Then Jake whirled at a sound beyond the door, his hand streaking down to come up with his Colt.

"No! It's only my boy!" Ann screamed. "No!"

Jake stood stiffly, the long barrel of the revolver aimed at Stevie in the doorway.

"What you doin' to my mommy?" the boy asked.

"It's all right, Stevie," his mother told him. "Your lunch is on the table. Go inside."

80

"You're bleeding. He hit you."

"It's all right, Stevie. It's all right. Go inside now."

"C'mere, kid," Jake Clinton said. He grinned at the ludicrous idea of the small boy so obviously determined to help the woman. "You come here."

Stevie inched away. "You bad man. When the marsh'l gets back, he'll fix you."

Jake's face tightened, hardened. Two long strides and he had Stevie's arm. "Where'd the marshal go?"

"Ow! My arm. You're hurtin' my arm!"

"Where'd he go?"

Stevie, whimpering, said, "Rode outta town early." His whimpers changed to crying.

Jake Clinton swung the boy toward the door and glared at Ann. "Get into the house with the kid," he ordered. "You try anythin' else, he gets it, too. Now go 'head. Git."

11

T HE SUN, LOW ABOVE THE western horizon, hadn't lost any of its driving heat, though the shadows slanting east had reached full length and the sandbars of the Platte had lost their dazzling white glare. There was no wind, not even a trace of cloud in the brassy sky, when McQuade crossed the river just a few minutes after four o'clock. He walked tiredly along the back of the business district and entered Appell's store through the rear door.

The interior was cool and pleasant, the sweet, faint odor of peppermint candy ticklish to McQuade's nose. The young clerk was waiting on a farmer and his wife at one end of the front counter. Appell was sitting behind a high-topped desk in the rear left corner, beyond shelves and counters bulging with shoes, clothing and dry goods. He looked up from the papers spread before him when he heard McQuade step out of the back storeroom.

Appell's eyes slid from McQuade's scraped forehead to the Winchester tucked under the arm of the lawman's dusty, sweat-stained shirt. The room's shadows accented the concerned expression on his round face. "There's been more trouble, Marshal?"

"Just what's been comin'." He quietly told Appell about the bushwhacker, ending with, "Whoever it was didn't want any questions asked about that cattle, Mayor."

"Could it have been the cowhand you kicked out of town? He had reason to hate you."

"He was a mile ahead when it happened. The bushwhacker was waiting for Frenchy, and he led me right into him."

The mayor stood slowly. He rubbed his thick jowls and glanced down to the other end of the long room. The clerk had finished with his customers, and now he was busy straightening out the display at the shirt counter.

Appell lowered his voice. "If you think you should have more deputies, I'll speak to the council."

McQuade shook his head. "Mayor, if I'm right about this, the men of Farmington couldn't handle what could happen. They'll be killers like Calem Voci, and they'll come in strong. The only way to stop them is to have that street out there empty, with so many guns covering the bank door anyone who rides in would see it's suicide to pull a robbery."

Worriedly, Appell gazed down at the papers on the desk. Without speaking, he rubbed his hand aimlessly across his jaw. After a minute he raised his eyes to McQuade.

"There's been too much planned. Too much depends on tomorrow. All the goods I've got stocked, all the supplies the other merchants have brought in are for the farmers."

"You'll have a small loss, but it'll be worth it."

"No. We can't take a loss," Appell said loudly. "We can't afford to." He paused, looking toward the clerk again. "We can't stop the plans now. It would ruin too many of the people here in town."

"The people? You haven't given them a choice. I can tell you about a holdup just like the one I think's being set up. The first thing the gunmen did was fire into the people on the streets. Two women and a kid were killed before the lawmen were smart enough to stop shooting and let the robbers ride out of town." McQuade jerked the Winchester at the street. "You ask the people if they want any part of something like that?"

Mayor Appell continued to stare at McQuade for a few seconds, all his worry clear in his face. Then he shook his head. McQuade wasn't sure whether it was a reproachful motion or whether what he'd said had found deeper understanding.

Appell said, "All right, Marshal. I'll talk to Stillwell and the council."

"I'll go with you if you want."

"No. No, I'll see them alone."

Nodding, McQuade turned and walked up the main aisle toward the porch. Outside, the wide street was thickly shadowed. Green shades had been drawn over the windows of the bank, one sign of the close of the workday. People moved about the walks at a leisurely pace, some of them grouped to look at the almost completed platform at lower Union. Others watched the men who were blocking off the

83

walks, tying from hitchrail to hitchrail the ropes that would hold the Wild West Show audience back from the street.

McQuade thought again of all the competent plans that had gone into tomorrow's affair. He dropped the thought when he became aware of the stringy man dressed in cowhand's clothing who was standing in the doorway of the hotel. Something in the way he was waiting, in the way he held the lower half of his body behind the doorjamb warned McQuade.

"McQuade! Hey there, McQuade!"

The call from ahead was unfriendly, more of an order. Seth Perrault was bustling toward him, his stubby arms flapping at his sides. McQuade's eyes didn't leave the hotel doorway as he slowed his walk.

"Dammit," Seth wheezed, panting from his short run, "You're a public servant, McQuade. A citizen calls you, you stop."

"I'm stopped," McQuade said. He shifted his stance a little, keeping the hostler on his right, placing his own body between the hotel and Seth.

"It's your horse," Seth began. "You got a barn behind the jail. I figure it's 'bout time you took him in there."

"All right. I'll have him moved before the morning."

"Before the mornin'. Dammit, you get him out 'fore then!"

"Get over—over!" McQuade turned completely around, catching the sound of quick movement he'd been listening for from the hotel porch. He swung wide with the Winchester, knocking Seth back in the motion of bringing up the weapon.

The tall cowhand was in plain view, six-guns held aimed in both hands. McQuade doubled over and threw his body to the dusty street. Two shots blasted the peacefulness of the town, and the bullets zinged hatefully over McQuade's head. Instantly he pushed himself to his elbow, pumping, firing the carbine once, twice.

The attacker's face twisted in shock. His body stopped, stiffening as though he'd smashed into a stone wall. One of his guns thundered again. The bullet went wild and ripped through a porch timber.

McQuade put a third slug into the gunman before he swayed and pitched forward. He landed on his face, then rolled awkwardly down the steps to the street.

Shoes and boots pounded on the walks. Men yelled

84

loudly, those who'd appeared in doorways calling questions to the people already outside. McQuade leaned over the fallen gunman. He was dead, blood reddening his shirt in three spots on his chest. McQuade had never seen him before.

McQuade's head jerked up, expecting more trouble as the lobby screen door slammed back and the old hotel clerk ran out. "Marshal! Two of them, Marshal!" he screamed. "There's two of them!"

"Where?"

"One went 'round the jail! 'Round back!"

McQuade had whirled before Millett finished. "Out of the way," he yelled to those who'd closed in between himself and the jail doorway. "Keep out of the way!"

The watchers scrambled for cover. From behind he heard Millett call, "Clinton! Their name's Clinton, Marshal!"

The office was empty, McQuade saw before he'd crossed the walk, and the door to the cell block was locked. He kept moving fast, through the office and out the rear door.

He was halfway across the empty yard when Ann appeared in the kitchen window. One of her hands pointed to the barn, and she called something, but her words were lost behind the glass.

The back door suddenly swung open wide, and Stevie stepped onto the porch. "The barn, Marsh'l. He's out back of the barn!"

"Back. Back in the house," McQuade called. He made out the figure of a man coming at him from inside the barn. His face was hidden in the deep shadows, but from the way he raised his right hand, McQuade knew he was holding an aimed gun.

The man's gun flashed, and a bullet seared through McQuade's coat. McQuade fired at the barrel flame and pumped out two quick shots as he shifted his stride to the left and the cover of the open door. He saw the shadowy figure fall to one knee, yet the gun inside spit fire again.

The bullet zinged past McQuade and smashed through the jail window. McQuade pressed his body against the rough boards of the barn. Loud, confused noise filled the interior, the high, frightened whinnies of the bay, the wild kicking of the trapped horse as it tried to break out of its stall.

Another shot blasted inside. This time it came from the rear of the building.

McQuade, holding fire, edged around the door. Daylight streaked in through the back entrance, but McQuade couldn't be positive the gunman had run. Crouching low, he made his dash for the closest stall, watching for another shot. He slid into the stall and waited there a moment, eyes and Winchester ready to catch a barrel flash.

No shot came, only the drumming of a horse's hoofs out in the side street.

McQuade reached the open rear doorway and hesitated long enough to listen for sound close by. He stepped into the brightness of the sunlight, knowing the gunman had gotten away. Behind him the bay still kicked against the stall. McQuade went back inside and spoke softly to the horse.

Stevie ran in from the yard. "You get him?" He halted in the open doorway. His eyes roamed up and down the aisle. "He was out there since mornin'! Waitin' for you t' get back!"

"You talked to him?"

"Yuh! He made me and Mommy stay in the house all day!"

Ann Heath entered the barn, and McQuade left the stall. Ann stared fearfully at her son. "You shouldn't've run out like that."

"We had to tell the marsh'l, Mommy. The man woulda killed him."

She gripped the boy's shoulder and started to turn him into the yard. McQuade asked, "Steve said you talked to that man. What did he look like?"

"He was tall and husky. With a heavy beard. He called the other one Ed."

Ann studied him, searching his scraped forehead as though in an effort to read his thoughts. Her hand trembled on her son's shoulder. Her eyes dropped. "Come back to the house, Stevie."

"He was a bad man," the boy blurted out. "He hit Mommy for tryin' to saddle our horse."

McQuade, going closer to Ann, could see the slight swelling at the corner of her mouth now. "You tried to ride out?"

"Yes, I tried," she said evenly. "I did a lot of thinking this morning, and I started to have some hope—" Men had crowded out of the alleyway, were thronging across the yard. Ann shook her head, added emotionally, "All I could think of was that day in Tombstone. I had to get that gunman away from the house before Stevie came home from school."

"I know," he said. "It was the right thing to do."

"It didn't have to be. I shouldn't have had to go through all this." She was pale and defiant, and he saw that her lower lip was shaking.

He wanted to talk more, but the crowd closed in on him, the excited men yelling questions, pushing, pressing to get into the interior of the barn. Over the heads of the crowd McQuade watched Ann take Stevie's hand and lead him toward the house. He sighed wearily. Then, paying no attention to the questions, he broke through the ring of watchers and started back to Union Street.

"They come into the hotel this mornin'," Millett said. The elderly clerk pointed to Ed Clinton's body. "This one hit me. Here, look at my face."

"Lookit Seth here," Tom Gruber shouted to the people crowded around. "He almost got killed. It ain't even safe to talk to McQuade, or you take a chance on gettin' killed."

Men in close to the hotel porch began grumbling. Billy Ford had made his way through to the dead man. McQuade came out of the jail and started across Union, and those in the rear stopped their talk as McQuade passed them. They wouldn't meet the lawman's eyes. Most of them stirred uncomfortably and looked down at their feet or felt their faces self-consciously.

Gruber, seeing their reaction, swore and called again wildly. "Look at Millett here. Look at how he got beat up!"

Mayor Appell, who'd just reached the crowd, grabbed Millett's arm. "They beat you?"

"This one did." The clerk raised one hand to his bruised nose. "When I saw them sign Clinton, I tried to get over to the jail." He spotted McQuade, and a worried stare covered his face. "You kill the other one, Marshal?"

"No. But I hit him before he got to his horse. They said they were Clintons?"

"That's right. Clinton!" He repeated the name loudly, so even those at the rear could hear.

McQuade felt the sudden dead silence. The tension that reached him from the watchers was almost as heavy as the thick shadows that darkened their faces. He gave the dead man a slow survey before he spoke.

"If he's a Clinton," he said, "I've never seen him before."

"They signed Clinton, though."

"This other man. Did he limp a little? His right leg?"

Millet frowned thoughtfully. "No. He signed Jacob Clinton. You can see the register." He tugged at McQuade's sleeve. "I'll show you."

Nodding, McQuade looked at Billy Ford. "Handle things here." He went along with the old clerk.

Billy motioned to the watchers in close to the body. "Here, you men. Help get him down to Doc's."

Only one of the men moved. Mayor Appell stepped to the dead man's feet and began to bend. But he straightened when Tom Gruber said, "What do we do now, Appell? Jest sit 'round and wait for the other Clinton to come back?"

"Look," Billy snapped. "Cut that talk."

"You shut up, Billy," a man on the porch shouted. "Let Tom have his say. All this is Appell's fault. He hired that gunslinger for marshal." And to Gruber, "You tell him, Grub. We're with you."

"What you gonna do 'bout it, Appell?" said Gruber.

"McQuade's the marshal. What can I do about it?"

"Fire him," a high-pitched voice called. "You can fire him."

Muttering and movement broke out, more curses in the talk now, obscene words that, despite the women and children present, no one tried to hold down.

"McQuade has a contract," Appell said.

"Gruber had a contract," the same voice yelled. "That's right," another man snarled. "Get rid of that killer and give Grub back his badge. What say, Grub? You take the marshal's badge?"

Gruber nodded. "You get the council to hire me."

"The council can't hire you or anyone else," Appell said. Not unless McQuade resigns." His eyes slid across the circle of faces. "I can't force him to resign. Which one of you wants to try it?"

The angry talk dwindled down to mumbling, but no one answered Appell's challenge. A few in the rear began to step away and return to their homes and families. The others watched Billy Ford and Appell lift the dead man. All of them were quiet now, and all possessed the same blank look of being trapped and not being able to do anything about it.

Gruber stayed close to Appell and said loudly, "Just the

same, Mayor, I'll take that job. You get rid of McQuade, I'll get this town back to where Ben Ford had it."

One mile west of Farmington Jake Clinton lay in the cool dampness of the scrub willows that lined the Platte's south bank. He was calm now, listening for a sound along the flat, but his breath still came heavily. Once he'd seen there was no one directly behind him, he'd dismounted and looked at his wound.

He'd never been shot before, had been surprised it hadn't started to hurt until after he'd gotten his second shot off. Even though McQuade's bullet had knocked him to one knee, it felt more like a big rock had hit him than a lead slug. The pain had come then, digging in like the burn of a white-hot iron, and he'd started to shake all over. That was when he'd panicked, forgetting Ed out in the street, the bank, the two brothers of his McQuade had killed in Tombstone.

He'd run. He'd ridden hard, intent only on getting safely away to fix his wound. It was a deep gash high up in the inside of his thigh, and it was bleeding badly. As long as he could press the vein that fed the wound, he was all right. Riding was out. He couldn't stand the jogging or loss of blood. And he couldn't keep his horse here.

He worked fast, taking off one spur, lifting the saddle a bit and shoving the spur underneath. He fell back fast, clear of the animal's first furious buck to stop the pain of the rowel digging into its back. Crying crazily, the horse crashed through the brush and racked off to the west. It would run until it was exhausted, and would lead a posse a good chase until then.

Jake didn't start to think about his cousin Ed until after he'd controlled his bleeding. Ed was badly wounded, he figured, maybe dead. His cousin was dead, and he'd run from the man who'd done it, the same man who'd killed his own two brothers.

He could never go back to Dingo and admit he'd run, that he'd left Ed alone back there. He couldn't stand up to English after the holdup and demand more of a cut, not when everyone knew he'd run. Jake Clinton lay quietly, feeling stronger now. He listened to the muted gurgle of the river over the long grayish sand bars, brushing away mosquitoes while he watched the fireflies flicker in the brush.

He made his decision to go back and see what had happened to Ed. If Ed was dead, he'd wait for his chance at McQuade. He might never get out of town, he knew, but there would be no life for him, anyway, if he didn't kill McQuade.

12

Henry Stillwell was halfway through supper when the gunfire started. Now the banker hurried along Union, past his neighbors, who were talking loudly in small groups on lawns or the porches of their houses. Stillwell could see the body of a man being carried toward lower Union. "Oh, my Lord," he muttered, then broke into a run, his black coat flapping behind him.

He saw George English coming through the crowd with bald Sid Davis. Both men looked worried. Their expressions didn't change when they met Stillwell.

"Do you hear the talk?" English asked. "The whole town has turned, Henry."

"I know. They can't seem to understand."

"What do you expect them to understand?" Davis said. "It's up to the council to do something." The scowl on his broad face became deeper, and he focused his eyes on English. "This's even got George down. He's thinking of leaving himself."

Stillwell stared at the newspaperman. "You should know better than to start talk like that."

English accepted the statement and nodded. "I'm thinking of Ann, Henry. You know what she's already been through. I'd rather leave with her than ask her to face all this trouble McQuade's brought in."

"There won't be any more trouble. We'll get rid of McQuade." Stillwell quieted and looked toward lower Union. Suddenly he pointed his index finger in that direction. "Appell. You, Appell! Get over here!"

The mayor, who'd just stepped from the doctor's house, halted momentarily to gaze at the three men. Quickly, he walked to where they stood.

Stillwell spoke before Appell reached them. "You see what's happening? What hiring that gunman has brought?

Those Clintons tried to kill McQuade once, and they'll try again."

"We're not positive they were Clintons," Appell told him. "McQuade said he'd never seen the dead one before."

"I don't care what McQuade said. They were gunmen, and they never would've come here if you hadn't brought McQuade in."

Both English and Davis nodded in agreement. "I believe they were Clintons," English said. "The trouble will last as long as McQuade stays."

"That's a change for you, George. You wanted to hire McQuade just as much as I did."

"Well, I don't want him now. I'm for getting rid of him before he brings us any more trouble."

"I don't know," said Appell. He drew a deep breath and exhaled while he stared along Union. McQuade had appeared from the hotel. He'd already stepped off the porch, and was crossing to his office. "I don't know," Appell repeated. "But as long as there's any threat of a holdup, I think we'd better cancel the show tomorrow."

Stillwell stared at the mayor, dumfounded. He swallowed, his tone rising. "We can't cancel. You know that."

"There'll be women and children out in this street. I don't want to be responsible for them."

"No. We get rid of your marshal, there'll be no danger. We won't cancel anything except our contract with McQuade."

"Just until Sunday, Henry. We can get Carson to stay over that long."

Stillwell paid absolutely no attention to that. His eyes were on McQuade, almost to the jail. "Are you coming with us or aren't you?"

"But we shouldn't take this much of a chance."

"We're asking McQuade to resign. Are you coming?"

"No. I won't be responsible, Henry."

"You won't have to be," Stillwell said coldly. He swung around and started for the opposite walk.

English and Davis fell in behind the banker, leaving Appell alone in the center of the dusty street.

Dan McQuade had seen the three men turn their backs on Appell, and he knew they were following him into his office. He stopped at his desk and turned to face the door.

Stillwell entered first, his flushed face held high, like an indignant rooster. The others halted beside him.

"Gentlemen?" asked McQuade.

"We're speaking for the citizens of Farmington," Stillwell said, his eyes narrowed and unfriendly. "We want you to resign as marshal."

"There has to be reason for resigning."

"Those gunmen were after you. You quit, it will keep men like them from coming to Farmington. You can't expect the people here to become part of your trouble with the Clintons."

"I know what I can expect of the people here, Mr. Stillwell."

The banker opened his mouth, but he closed it again when Billy Ford appeared in the doorway holding the dead man's twin gunbelts in his hand. Billy halted when he noticed the council members.

"No identification at all on that one." He held out the gunbelts to McQuade. "Not even initials burned in."

"Both of you are still here, McQuade." Stillwell smiled, yet the hard expression around his eyes didn't change.

McQuade took the gunbelts and studied them without a word.

Stillwell added pointedly, "They tried to kill you, McQuade. I'd think you'd be going after the one who got away."

McQuade looked up, met the banker's stare. "A posse?" He smiled coldly and picked up the challenge. "You're willing to be in on it—all of you?"

Stillwell shook his head. "No. No, you don't. You don't drag us into your private fights."

"There's nothing private about a shootout in your own main street."

Davis grunted loudly. "Damn all this talk!" He jabbed a bony finger at McQuade. "You heard Millett say who them gunmen were. You ought to have the decency to get out of Farmington until it's settled."

"I ought to have the decency," McQuade mimicked. "I ought to do just what you want and resign. And let you face what's coming. If it was only you who'd suffer, I might do that." He dropped the six-guns on the desk with a loud thud. "I ought to kick your butts right out of this office."

Davis, jerking his finger back, said nothing more. Stillwell sputtered, but it was English who answered McQuade. "Then you won't resign."

"No, I'm not resigning. I'm not taking any posse out on any long chase that'll leave this town wide open. I've got a contract, and I'll stay as long as it's legal."

"We'll see about that," Stillwell said, his hot, furious eyes touching English and Davis. "We'll see about that," he repeated, then swung around and strode from the room.

Davis followed behind the banker, but English hesitated. The newspaperman's eyes were clearer than usual, but completely calm.

"Marshal, I voted for you, but now I know I was wrong," he said. He took a deep breath and let it out carefully. "You know about me and Mrs. Heath, and you know what all this trouble is doing to her. I'm getting her and the boy out of town. I'm afraid of what you can cause here tomorrow."

"That's up to you," McQuade replied. "You do what you think is right."

The newspaperman's face became strained. "There will be others who won't want to take chances. You see them leaving, too, you'll know why." He turned and went outside.

McQuade walked to the doorway and stood there looking out. One hand rubbed absently along his jawbone as his gaze followed English. In the silence, Billy Ford spoke.

"This town means a lot to Mr. English," he said stiffly.

"Not enough—not when he starts to pack the first time things get rough."

Billy suddenly swore and said with a bitter smile, "You know all the answers. You're so damned sure."

"Yes, I am sure," McQuade answered, still studying the street. "You doubt me, you can turn in that badge."

The deputy's face reddened. Disgustedly, he wiped one hand across his mouth. "I'll make this round before I go out to Hanley's place for my girl."

McQuade glanced around. "Your girl will have to get in herself. Neither of us leaves town."

"Look, Marshal. We made plans for the dance."

"Don't leave town," McQuade said. "One of those bush-whackers got away. He could be waiting for us to follow him. You'd be a sitting duck with that star on."

"But she'll be waitin' for me."

94

"Have one of your friends tell her why you can't go out. She thinks you're worth it, she'll come in on her own." McQuade walked back to the desk and picked up the gunbelts.

Billy stood tensely for almost a minute. Finally, muttering something under his breath, he jerked his sombrero low over his eyes and started from the office.

"Watch it there," McQuade said after him.

The deputy didn't answer and gave no sign he'd heard.

"I said watch it!" McQuade snapped. "That bushwhacker could come back in here. You'd be number two target."

Billy's back stiffened as he passed through the doorway, but he didn't stop. He kept on walking.

Tom Gruber was worried and afraid. He'd gone into the *Tribune* office through the back entrance following the gunfight, and now he watched English as the newspaperman approached along the walk. The tight, serious lines on English's handsome face told Gruber he was worried, too, and that made him even more fearful.

Gruber didn't move from the back of the room until English came inside. He started to speak as soon as the door closed, but English motioned him silent.

Quickly English drew the shade. "Get out, you damn fool," he snapped. "Seth Perrault's coming."

"What do I do, Mr. English? Do we still—"

"Nothing's changed. I'll get in touch with you later. Get going."

Gruber's hand touched the doorknob. He didn't have time to turn it before the front door swung back and the skinny hostler stepped inside.

Seth halted in the open doorway, his eyes on Gruber. "Oh, I didn't expect you'd be in here, Tom."

Gruber's fingers slipped from the knob. He began to stammer something, but English spoke up. "Mr. Gruber just stopped in to see about this week's edition. He was just leaving. Come in, Seth."

The hostler closed the door, his gaze still a little doubtful, still on Gruber. "Well—it's that gunfight," he said to English. "I thought maybe you'd like the whole story for your paper." He paused when Gruber opened the door. "You don't have to go, Tom."

"Yeah, I better go," Gruber said. "I gotta see Appell about how the people talked out there."

"There's a chance Tom'll get the marshal's job," English explained. "That's partly why he was in here."

"Damned right," Seth said. "That whole thing was McQuade's fault."

"Sure," Gruber nodded. "You tell Appell, too. Tell him later." Gruber stepped outside and closed the door behind him.

A nervous sweat had broken out all over his body, and even in the sultry heat he felt cold and clammy. He'd made a mistake waiting there, and he dreaded finding out what English might do about it. He'd gotten in on the holdup plan partly to get even for what the town had done to him and partly because he wanted the marshal's job. He hadn't really realized how ruthless English could be, not until English had come back from his meeting with Jake Clinton.

He'd learned how McQuade was to be killed, how the gang would fire into the crowd if they had to. He couldn't back out by then, he didn't dare to . . .

The sun had already set in the west, and the hazy summer dusk that seemed to come off the Platte had descended in a soft, bluish darkness over the town. Lights had gone on in all the buildings along Union. As he crossed toward the hotel he could see the shadows of the drinkers behind the half-frosted glass of the saloon. Gruber stepped up onto the walk to the left of the porch and began to ascend the steps.

"Hey, you, Gruber," a voice whispered from the alleyway beside the hotel.

Gruber froze and stared into the dark shadows. He could see the tall form pressed close to the building and knew it was Jake Clinton seconds before he could distinguish his face.

Gruber side-stepped into the darkness. "What you doin', comin' back here?"

"Shut up!" Clinton snapped in a low, strained voice. He bent over painfully, his right hand grabbing at his thigh. He grunted and held on tightly. "You gotta fix me up."

"I can't do anythin' for you. Look, Mr. English—"

"Get me some water and bandages. Quick, dammit."

Gruber glanced out at Union. He thought of English, then remembered that Seth Perrault was in the *Tribune* office. The walks were clear close by, but a woman and man who'd left the hardware store were headed his way.

"Look, I can't take a chance on bein' seen with you. What if we get caught?"

"We won't get caught. You gotta fix this leg or I'll bleed to death." Clinton cursed, leaning all his weight against the side of the hotel for support.

Silently, Gruber studied the street again, his cold nervousness warming to calm thought. "Go 'round the back door. I'll let you in."

Clinton nodded and, bent way over, staggered toward the rear of the building.

Gruber returned to the walk. The hotel porch was empty. Quickly, he went to the rear door of the lobby and unlocked it. He could read the pain in Jake Clinton's chalk-white face the moment he let him in and began hurrying him down the corridor.

Inside his room, Gruber drew the shade before he lit the wall lamp. Clinton sat on the bed and started to tear open his bloodied jeans. Gruber went to unbuckle the wounded man's gunbelt.

"No." Clinton snarled, pushing the hand away roughly. He had more strength than Gruber had believed, and was in better shape than he'd thought.

"I've got to get to the wound and clean it out."

"It's low down," Clinton said. He ripped the cloth clear of the bullet hole and leaned back on his elbows. "Just wash away the blood and bandage it."

"I've got extra pants. You can get into them."

"Come on, do what I say."

Gruber took the water basin from the dresser, then tore the pillowcase into wide bandages before he washed the wound. The bullet had gone through the flesh and gored a deep hole coming out. Gruber pressed along the bone to check if it had been broken or splintered.

Clinton trembled. "Okay. Okay, get the bandage on. I want to get back to the street."

"You should take it easy. Stay in here."

Clinton, glowering, flexed his right hand to keep the fingers nimble. "McQuade'll be out in the street. I want one more crack at him."

"Everyone knows who you are," Gruber told him. "McQuade's about through here. They're holdin' a meetin'

97

during the dance to vote him out. I'll be marshal after that. There won't be no worry about tomorrow."

Clinton shook his head and his voice was pinched with hate. "I want McQuade, and I'm going to get him. All I got to do is lay in that alley and wait for him to cross over to the dance." He flexed his fingers again. "Bandage it tight, so I can walk."

"Wait. I'll set things up. First I'll tell Mr. English you're here."

The protest was cut off as Clinton cursed obscenely.

"You tell English nothin'. You get this leg fixed, and let me rest a little while."

Gruber obeyed and went on bandaging the wound in silence.

13

DAN MCQUADE LET HIMSELF BE outlined plainly against
the lamplit doorway of his office. During the first half-hour
of prairie darkness, the townspeople had gradually appeared
on the walks, but they'd paid little attention to McQuade.
They'r moved past the jail without looking his way as they
went toward Granger Hall to admire the decorations and
to chat with each other about the evening's festivities.

McQuade was conscious of every face that passed,
every movement, but his thoughts centered on what he
couldn't see. Anyone who was after him could be
watching. The best way to draw that person out was to
keep out in the open. He moved from the doorway and
across the road to Appell's store.

He studied the street and alleyways, the yellow beams
of lamplight falling into Union from a hundred windows.
He felt the cold loneliness of a hated and hunted man
while his eyes flickered beyond Granger Hall to the irregu-
lar outlines of the buildings edging the town, standing tall
and black against the lesser darkness of the Nebraska
night.

Inside the store three men stood around the cracker
barrel with Appell. When McQuade entered their talk
ceased.

Appell walked to where McQuade had stopped near the
door, his eyes still on the street. "The gunfight has everyone on their nerves," Appell told him. "I've had nothing
but complaints."

"That figures," said McQuade. As soon as he'd come
inside more people had appeared from the side streets,
most of them adults accompanied by their children. "You
spoke about canceling the show, Mayor?"

"I tried. But the gunfight spoiled everything. I've got to
have time before I try again." His words came too quickly, too nervously.

McQuade nodded but didn't answer. He pushed the door open and went out on the porch.

The walks were crowded now, and small groups had gathered here and there to talk. Parents scolded with little success as boys shouted and romped among the grownups, wrestling, laughing, teasing. McQuade cut straight across to the jail, taking care to avoid the groups. If trouble came, he wanted no innocent bystander killed or wounded.

He'd reached the jail walk when Ann Heath and English came out of the alleyway leading to the house. She was more beautiful than he'd ever seen her, in a low-cut blue dress that showed off her smooth neck, and she'd unpinned her blond hair, allowing it to wave softly about her shoulders. McQuade started to hesitate so they'd pass close to him, his pulse hammering in his throat, but, remembering the danger, he continued on to the office.

They came abreast of him. English tipped his hat slightly, and for a moment McQuade felt Ann's fine hazel eyes rest on his face, then look ahead. He nodded, feeling that same poignant sense of loss strong in his mind.

From north of Depot, the first farmer's wagon rumbled into Union, driven by a bearded homesteader dressed in a high white collar and black coat. His wife and children were busy waving and calling to their friends as they rode past.

Two townsmen who stood in front of the hardware store spoke to the farmer while he tied his team to the rail. One was skinny, with a long pointed nose. His voice carried deliberately back to McQuade.

"We want every farmer at the meetin', too. You farmers are as much a part of this as anyone."

McQuade's face didn't change. He saw that Ann's back had stiffened at the words, but she didn't turn. McQuade moved from the doorway, back into the silence of his office.

He waited longer than twenty minutes, until the dance was in full swing, before he showed himself again. Laughter and talk mixed with the strains of *Turkey in the Straw*. McQuade went on to the boardwalk, pausing there to look at the hall's brightly lit windows and the townpeople who'd come out onto the porch for air. He'd stay at this end of Union, he decided, close to the road's center. He started slowly west, expecting anything . . .

The shots came in the moment he stepped down to the street, two shots suddenly exploding from the alleyway between the hotel and barbershop. A bullet sliced across the top of McQuade's left ear, ripping the Stetson off his head. The second slug tore through his coat and splintered the office window behind him.

McQuade threw himself to the right and fell flat, blood streaming down the side of his face as he drew his Colt. A third shot blasted from the alleyway. Hot steel zinged by, inches above McQuade's head, with a high, whining noise.

McQuade squeezed the trigger once, twice, and got both bullets off at the spot where he'd seen the barrel flash. He rolled fast to the left and pushed himself up. Once on his feet he began a zigzagging dash for the cover of the buildings across Union.

All music had ceased abruptly. Men piled out of Granger Hall, the clatter of their boots and shoes loud to McQuade.

"Inside! Inside!" he shouted their way. "Stay inside!"

He stumbled going onto the walk and fell hard against the corner of the barbershop. Pausing, he pressed on his ear and felt the warm blood flow through his fingers. With the moonlight blocked by the height of the buildings, he could see only night ahead. Cautiously, he slid around the corner.

At the far end of the alleyway a gun flashed. The bullet whacked into the clapboards two inches beyond McQuade's shoulder. He bent over and fired twice, aiming low in case the bushwhacker was crouching, too.

An obscene curse came from the black darkness, followed by the scuffling noise of a boot being dragged through sand. McQuade let his fifth bullet go at the sound, jumped across the width of the alley and pressed his body against the solid wood of the hotel.

No gunfire answered, only softer, more settled scuffling.

Yells came from the street, the sound of many feet loud out there. Someone inside a hotel room behind McQuade lighted a lamp. The bright beam sliced down into the alley, making McQuade and everything within ten feet of him visible in its spotlight glare.

Savage fear gripped McQuade. He crouched even lower, trying to escape the light. A single shot thundered from the blackness before he'd moved two feet.

McQuade's body was stopped in the middle of his

stride, then sent reeling back from the impact of the slug that smashed through his left side. He fell heavily, doubled over, gasping to regain the wind that had been knocked out of him by the bullet's sledge-hammer blow.

14

JAKE CLINTON LIMPED FORWARD TO close in on
McQuade, his six-gun aimed low for a make-sure shot. He
saw the blood streaking the side of McQuade's face and
the blood on his hand. Clinton's crazy laughter rang out
and echoed off the buildings. But he stopped suddenly and
looked toward the street.

McQuade gagged in his effort to regain his breath. He'd
heard the close shouts of the townspeople, just as Clinton
had heard them. In the second Clinton hesitated,
McQuade swallowed air. He forgot the pain in his side
and pushed out violently with his right arm, rolling his
body to the left.

Clinton's gun blasted. The bullet kicked up dirt where
McQuade's head had been.

The running, yelling mob reached the alleyway. Those
at the front moved into the thick darkness, forced ahead
by the men behind them. Clinton didn't fire another shot.
He whirled around and vanished in the night.

McQuade raised himself up onto one knee. He tried to
stand, but the intense pain that slashed down his side
made him stop. Quickly, he grabbed at his ribs and held
on tight to check the blood. He stood slowly, his back to
the men who crowded the alley. Once he was upright, his
head cleared a little.

"Hey, McQuade's hit," a man called. "He's hit. Look,
he's hit!"

Other voices joined in, yelling, questioning. Before they
reached him, McQuade had stepped into the blackness
that had swallowed up Jake Clinton.

McQuade kept close to the hotel's side, using the building more for support than for cover. At the rear entrance
he halted and stood absolutely still. He heard nothing out
ahead, only the chatter and quick, excited talk going on
behind him. He waited for another few seconds, making

103

certain Clinton wasn't close before he tried to round the corner and emerge from the deep shadows into the moonlight.

Heavy footsteps pounded behind him. Billy Ford, his .44 in his hand, crowded in next to McQuade.

"How many?" Billy asked.

"One. Jake Clinton. Keep those people back."

"You hit bad? They said you were hit."

"No. Only scraped my ear." McQuade let go of his side and raised his hand to his ear. The dirt and dust had clotted the wound, stopping the blood. He held the elbow in against his ribs, feeling the relief that came with the return of pressure. "Get those people clear."

Billy moved away. McQuade, edging around the corner, saw no sign of movement. Jake Clinton would've had a horse close by, he knew. At least Clinton would have a way out in case he needed it.

McQuade backed carefully alongside the hotel. He felt dizzy, that he might vomit, but he increased the pressure of the elbow against his side. The people would see the blood on his face and coat, and he wanted them to believe it came from his ear. He walked slowly past the more daring of the men, who'd come as far as the lamplight.

"Marshal, Billy told us it was Jake Clinton. That right?" Seth Perrault called. Another watcher picked up the question and added his remarks, but his words were drowned out by the noise of the men who were chattering loudly and shoving in on him to get nearer.

"Hey, that right, Marsh'l?" a farmer repeated. "That was Jake Clinton?"

Mayor Appell materialized from the hazy light in front of McQuade. "You shot, Marshal? They said you were shot."

McQuade nodded but continued up the alleyway.

The unruly talk got louder. McQuade looked into angry, outraged faces and heard the yell. "Hell, it's McQuade's fight then, not ours! Dammit! Hey you, Appell! I say you and your council get rid of him!" More shouts and hate-filled, violent cursing.

McQuade's dizziness returned. His side felt like a huge swollen thing that throbbed with a terrible fury, sending knife thrusts of pain through his chest. He couldn't go back and help Appell. He couldn't argue, couldn't speak for himself now, not until he fixed his side.

He walked slowly, keeping to the middle of the alley-way, both hands at his side. Those in close remained pressed tightly together for a few seconds, as though they meant to hold him. But then they opened a path to let him through.

The word about McQuade spread like brushfire along the porch of Granger Hall. When Ann Heath heard it she left the women and started off the steps. Dan was shot, perhaps badly ... Once in the street she broke into a run; she couldn't help herself. She didn't slow down until she was among the men lining the walk. She worked her way through, her heart beating wildly.

Dan was alone, almost to the marshal's office. She saw the blood on the side of his face and ran faster. From the head of the hotel alleyway a large crowd of men appeared, a loud, excited group with everyone yelling at once. They had Mayor Appell in the middle, and were taking their fear and anger out on him.

Ann circled wide behind the crowd of men to the jail. McQuade had stopped at the rolltop desk, his back to her.

"Dan . . ."

McQuade looked around, stared at her with eyes filled with pain and weariness. Swallowing, he dropped his elbow from his side. "I'm all right. You'd better get out."

"Your ear, Dan. I'll get water and a bandage."

"Just let me sit. I'll be all right." The words came hard, through gritted teeth.

He stepped back to the swivel chair. As he sat his coat opened, and Ann caught sight of his blood-soaked shirt. She gasped. "Your side, too. I'll get the doctor."

"No. If there's anyone watching for Clinton, they'll see how bad I'm hit. He'll come back tonight." He became silent and looked through the window into the street.

The crowd had crossed Union from the hotel alleyway, all the men gathered together like a mob. Appell and Stillwell were in front. Gruber and long-faced Seth Perrault were there, too. One farmer had lagged behind to shout to those on the porch of Granger Hall. Another man chased the young boys who were trailing the crowd back to their mothers.

Ann took a step to close the door.

"Leave it open," McQuade said. "Let them come."

"You can't face them. Not like this."

"Let them come in. Don't tell anyone—Appell, Stillwell, not even your brother."

McQuade pulled his body closer to the desk and straightened in the chair. Pain numbed his whole side, but his brain was clear. The pressure of his elbow seemed to have stopped the blood seeping from the wound.

The men in the lead came into the office. The rest crowded the doorway or spread out along the walk to peer through the window, their noses pressed flat against the glass. Stillwell halted opposite the desk.

"We want your badge," he ordered. "Everyone here has had enough of your gunfighting."

McQuade's gaze shifted to Appell. He said slowly, "You going along with this?"

Appell nodded. He would not meet McQuade's stare, and could not keep his eyes steady. "The people won't listen. You're wounded. You can't face anything wounded."

"It's just my ear, Mayor. It can be fixed easy enough."

"Like hell, Mayor," a man called from the doorway. "He's through right now. You tell him." A loud rumble of agreement ran through the watching men.

"We want your resignation," Stillwell said. "We've got our own man. Tom Gruber will fill in until we can settle your contract." He glanced toward the movement in the doorway and saw that Billy Ford had made his way inside. "These people want a marshal who isn't being hunted by every gunman within a thousand miles."

"You've told the people about the money you're bringing in tomorrow?" McQuade asked flatly. "You've given them a chance to decide on that, Mr. Stillwell?"

The banker stiffened at the outbreak of talk that followed. Before he could answer, Gruber said, "I'm takin' that badge, McQuade. I've got the council behind me."

"You'll get this badge only one way, mister."

The tense silence that rose lengthened while Gruber stood glaring down at McQuade. Then faint conversation began on the walk. The swelling of voices became higher, the mention of the word 'money' repeated loudly in the talk.

"You crazy killer," Gruber snarled. "You can't hold that badge with a gun."

"Get out," McQuade told them coldly. "All of you. Out."

Stillwell flared. "See here—"

106

"No, Mr. Stillwell. I'm not seeing anything as long as there will be women and kids out there tomorrow. You tell these people, Mr. Stillwell. Let them decide for themselves."

"Your talk could cause panic, McQuade. You've no right spreading talk like that."

"Maybe it'll keep the people inside. That'll be all I want."

More of the listeners pushed through the doorway to hear better. Stillwell exhaled heavily and studied the anxious faces. "Very well," he said. "But you're through. I'll take this to Omaha if I have to."

McQuade said nothing. He simply straightened a bit and watched the men who stood opposite him. Stillwell swung around and started out, and Appell, Gruber and the others followed. When they reached the walk the townspeople crowded in on Stillwell. Their talk was loud, demanding that the banker explain about the money.

Billy Ford said to McQuade, "Clinton couldn't have gone far yet. There's a chance of catching him."

McQuade shook his head. "We stay here. We don't leave town."

"He was alone. There's a chance that you hit him."

"No. I want you to stay inside that building opposite the bank for the night. In case someone tries getting in before morning to wait for that money." McQuade's eyes warned Billy. "You see anything, come get me. Don't stick your neck out alone."

Billy nodded and went outside.

Worriedly, Ann said, "I've got water and bandages, Dan. Come back to the house."

McQuade, shaking his head, watched her step toward the rear door. Again he straightened in the chair. "I'll come," he said. "After they break up."

Stillwell spoke to the crowd, but only snatches of what he said were audible in the office. The murmur and movement of the listeners died as the banker's talk calmed them. Three minutes later he had the people almost completely quiet. McQuade, watching without moving, held back the waves of dizziness that came as the first few men turned away and headed off to their families.

McQuade tried to stand, but when dizziness swept over him he sat down fast, waiting a little longer . . .

107

Ann Heath stepped from her kitchen onto the porch, then stood there worriedly. She heard the scrape of a shoe in the yard and immediately recognized the tall form of the man who was approaching the steps.

"George?"

"Ann, I thought you'd stayed safe on the porch," said George English. "When I saw you go into the jail, I—I didn't go in with those men because you were in there."

"Dan was shot. I couldn't just stand and wait." She started off the porch to go past him. English didn't move aside. "Ann, I realize you've been concerned. But McQuade's all right now."

"He'll need to clean up. I've put some water on. If it was Billy, I'd do the same thing."

English nodded. "I understand, dear."

She remained close to him and kissed him softly. "I know you do. That's what I depend on. It's one reason I feel about you as I do."

He smiled, his face brightening. His hands gripped hers, firmly but tenderly. "I'd begun to get worried. There was a time when you felt about McQuade like— I wasn't certain you couldn't have a change of mind."

For a moment her face was devoid of expression, but then she shook her head. "I haven't changed about that, George. I'll be ready for the train tomorrow."

When she left English near the marshal's office, he was smiling and showing nothing except a calm, understanding exterior. Alone in the alleyway, his face contorted and he cursed. He knew the full danger of Ann's being too close to McQuade. The instant he'd seen her following McQuade into his office, a rage had flared inside him.

He'd been so positive where Ann was concerned, he hadn't worried. He wasn't so certain now. In that instant of rage, he'd thought only of Ann, and he knew he could kill McQuade himself—the loss of the railroad money, a jail term, hanging, the penalty be damned.

He was almost to the *Tribune* office when he heard his name called behind him. He looked back. It was Seth Perrault.

"McQuade refused to quit, Mr. English," the hostler said, falling in beside the newspaperman. "What can we do now?"

"I don't know. Actually, it's up to Appell."

"But Appell's so weak. It's up to men like you, Mr.

English. You and the rest of the council." He followed English into the *Tribune* office, and to the rear of the long room.

English was quiet as he struck a match and put it up to the overhead lamp. The flame touched the wick, and light flickered through the office. "You'll have to see Appell, Seth. I can't . . . "

The sound of a boot scraping the floor stopped his words, and together they looked to the left. Jake Clinton was sitting on the floor behind the large news press, a cocked and aimed six-gun in his hand.

Seth's eyes stared at Clinton's bloody pants leg. "Mr. English, he's Ja—"

"Who's he?" Clinton asked calmly. The barrel shifted inches, to Seth's chest.

"No! No!" Seth whimpered.

"Don't, you fool," English snapped. "One shot and the whole town will be in here."

Seth edged away from the two men, his eyes wide, as he looked at English. He didn't quite understand, but it wouldn't take long before he did. One of his hands gripped the doorknob and began to turn it.

English turned to his desk and jerked open the top drawer. Before Seth had the door pulled all the way back, English was holding a stubby double-barreled Remington derringer aimed at him.

"Back in, Seth. I want to—"

"No." His eyes flicked to Clinton, returned to English. "You won't shoot." He started through the doorway.

English moved after him but hesitated when Clinton waved the revolver. "Take this. Something that'll give you distance."

The six-gun felt heavy to English as he went out into the darkness. He dashed along the rear of the building, tracking the noise of Seth's running feet, knowing everything could end right here, right now, if Seth reached the street.

In the alleyway he made out Seth's silhouette, dark against the lamplight of Union. "Seth! Hold it, Seth!"

The hostler looked around and slowed. "Seth," English called. "Wait . . ." Seth halted, ten feet from the mouth of the alley. "I had to make it look good, Seth. I had to go along with that killer so you could get out."

Seth faced English. "I knew there was something, Mr.

109

English. I knew." He grinned confidently. "Now, we'd better—"

He never finished, for English brought the heavy steel barrel down on his head violently, knocking the hostler senseless.

Wildly, English kept swinging the gun's barrel, smashing it into the hostler's face and head even after Seth was dead. After he stopped, he stood silently against the side of the *Tribune* building, listening to see if anyone had been attracted by the commotion.

Shortly, satisfied no one would discover him, English bent over and began dragging Seth's limp body back toward the foot of the alleyway.

Ann saw McQuade's weakness clearly when he finally stood. She moved along close beside him as he walked out the rear door, but she didn't try to take his arm until they were in the dark.

McQuade stumbled at the bottom porch step. Ann held on tightly and kept him from falling. Once inside, she led him to the downstairs bedroom her father had used. Gently, she took off his coat. He'd lost a lot of blood. His shirt and the top of his pants were soaked with it.

McQuade took out the makings and rolled a cigarette. Ann waited until he sat back, more relaxed while he smoked, before she went into the kitchen. McQuade laid his head on the pillow and listened to her shake the stove and work the pump, splashing water into a pan. After three minutes she returned with a bowl of steaming water, bandages and an armful of towels.

"Roll onto your side, Dan."

Ann fixed his ear first, a small cut that bled little while she cleaned and bandaged it. Then she took a pair of scissors and cut through his shirt. Tenderly, she examined the wound, her slim fingers feeling about with extreme care. The bullet had ripped a gash an inch long just below the lower rib, going in and coming out almost in the same spot. The pressure of his elbow had allowed the blood to coagulate, but a sudden movement could reopen the hole.

"You should have a doctor," she said.

"No. No doctor."

"It could open up. You've lost too much blood already."

McQuade began pushing himself up onto his left elbow

110

to look at the wound, but as pain tore along his whole side he dropped back on the softness of the pillow and shook his head. "No. I don't want anyone to know. Not anyone."

"But you can trust Doctor Webster."

"Someone in this town's set up the bank, Ann."

"You're not positive, Dan. You can't . . ."

"I'm sure. Very sure. It could be anyone. More than one. You'll fix me up all right. Just bandage it good and tight." He exhaled deeply and closed his eyes.

The hot water dug deep, but it was soothing. For more than a quarter hour Ann cleaned the wound. She used most of the time to probe and pick out pieces of shirt, easing up when McQuade's big body trembled or the muscles in his side stiffened under her careful hands.

After the bandage was on, she straightened and looked down at McQuade. "It's clean. But it's so deep I really should get the doctor."

"Later. When the show's over."

"Oh, Dan. If only you'd—" She fell silent, her eyes troubled while she studied his face. "You're hurt. The town has turned against you. There's no reason why you should stay. You don't owe anyone this much."

"The law does." He rubbed the cigarette out in the bone ash tray on the bedside table, then pushed himself up to a sitting position, his body shivering at the effort. "The women and kids aren't responsible for what the men do. The law owes them protection."

Ann nodded. She became pensively silent, then asked in a soft voice, "What'll you do? After, I mean?"

"I'm not sure. It's different here. In Arizona a man can stay around knowing he's needed, even if he isn't wanted. Here—I don't know."

She waited for another moment. Finally, she turned. "I'll get coffee."

He did not answer, and she left the room. While Ann boiled more water, she looked at the bed and saw he had lain back again. When she walked to the bed she found he was asleep. She stared at the bloodstained sheet, the bandages on his side and head and the strained lines of his face. Quietly, she turned the lamp low and pushed her father's overstuffed chair beside the bed.

For a long while she sat there so she'd be near if he woke up and needed her. She felt close to McQuade now, as close as she had felt just before she left Tombstone. She'd been the weak, injured one then, and she'd run. But he'd never run, he'd never quit.

She sat quietly, thinking and listening to the sound of his heavy breathing, looking at his broad muscled shoulders and back, at the hair she wanted to touch, to push away from his forehead.

15

When McQuade awoke the sun hadn't yet risen above the horizon, but it was getting light. The night's coolness hugged the land, and the prairie air outside the window was still and fresh. McQuade's bandaged ear felt fine. He pushed himself up straight. He still felt weak, but his side didn't throb with that slow, steady rhythm.

McQuade stood carefully, aware of the pulling sensation along his ribs. For the next minute he held onto the iron bedpost. It helped settle the shakiness that died with the return of his strength.

The low rattle of a stove being opened sounded beyond the closed kitchen door. McQuade took his gunbelt from the dresser and buckled it on. The Colt seemed very heavy, and the weight of it dragged at his side. He stood still until the throbbing stopped. When he opened the door, the warm smell of coffee filled the kitchen. Ann turned at the stove, her face tired, concerned.

"You should get more rest, Dan."

"The train'll be comin' in." He pulled back a chair to sit.

Ann didn't answer. She poured some coffee into a mug and set it in front of him. "This'll help."

"Thanks, Ann." He looked at her, not drinking. "Ann, you wouldn't know Tombstone now. A man can raise his family and run his business without having to worry about his woman and kids. It's different, Ann."

She nodded but didn't meet his stare. She looked away, at the door behind him. "I ironed one of my father's shirts. And one of his suits is in the closet."

Nodding slowly, he said, "I'll keep this suit. I change now, there'd be questions asked."

"You'll need a tie, anyway." Ann went into the bedroom.

McQuade swallowed a mouthful of coffee and felt its

good warmth all through his body. The yellow-violet sparkle of sunlight crawled across the yard outside and beamed in through the window. He stood, took the shirt from the hanger and moved to the window. Here and there in the vast sweep of sky a few small clouds dotted the blue. Nothing else seemed to move over the endless stretch of Nebraska flat.

Then he noticed the small line of black smoke near the eastern horizon. He heard footsteps in the yard, and he turned to face the porch.

Billy opened the door. He was hatless, his collar unbuttoned, eyes puffy from loss of sleep. "Train's comin' in," he said. He stared at McQuade's shirt with a queer expression and added, "I figured you'd want to be down there."

"Good. I'll be right out."

Billy didn't move. He inspected the coffee cup on the table, and then his eyes flicked to the closed bedroom door, suspicion showing plainly now.

"Ann," he said. "Ann?"

"Yes, Billy?" His sister pushed open the door. She held a pillow in her hands, fluffing it.

Billy's eyes snapped to McQuade. "What is this?"

"Hold it," McQuade said. "You've got the wrong idea."

"Don't tell me." Billy's square face twisted angrily. "Don't tell me about Clinton tryin' to get into that bank during the night."

"Billy." Ann let the pillow drop onto the unmade bed. "I don't like what you're thinking."

"I don't either." He glared hatefully at McQuade. "Some men dirty everything they touch." Suddenly he swore and started for McQuade, his big fists swinging at his sides.

"Billy!" Ann called. She tried to move in between the two men, but she was too slow. "Billy!"

A sweeping roundhouse right connected with McQuade's head before he could duck. McQuade went down, doubled up, gasping from pain, trying to get a mouthful of air. Billy towered in on him and bent to yank McQuade to his feet.

"No! No!" Ann screamed. "Let him go, Billy!"

"Yellow," Billy growled. "You filthy, yellow gunman."

"He's hurt, Billy! He was shot in the side, too!" Ann grabbed her brother's arm and pointed to the trash box behind the stove. She picked out the remains of

114

McQuade's shirt and held the torn, bloody cloth for Billy to see. "One of those bullets hit his side."

Billy stared down at McQuade, who was pushing himself painfully to his knees. Billy wet his lips. "I thought . . ."

"He rested here, that's all." Ann's face had drained white. She leaned close to help McQuade stand.

Her brother watched McQuade, on one knee now, still doubled over holding his injured side.

"I didn't know about his side. I didn't, Ann."

"Meet the train," McQuade said. "Be out there so the town can see you."

Billy hesitated awkwardly.

"Meet,it, I said. You're representing the law there."

For a second the deputy gazed helplessly at his sister. Then, without a word, he swung around and went outside.

McQuade was on his feet. His long frame shuddered as he sat down, but sitting didn't relieve the hot thumping of his wound.

"Let me see, Dan," Ann offered. "I'll fix the bandage."

"No. I'll be all right by the time the train gets in."

The hall door opened. Stevie, dressed in pajamas, stepped into the kitchen, both his hands rubbing sleep from his eyes. "Some noise woke me up," he said to his mother.

"Oh—well, it wasn't anything," she explained. "I was going to wake you early anyway."

Stevie, saying nothing, looked at McQuade. The lawman nodded to the boy and stood. From far off he could hear the chuffing of the train. Beyond the storage sheds at the east end of town, the engine poured great clouds of black smoke into the sky.

"We're leavin' this mornin'," Stevie told McQuade. "We're not going to see the cowboys and Indians."

"They might stop in Omaha," McQuade said. "They'll have a bigger show there." He went into the bedroom for his coat and Stetson. When he came out, Stevie spoke up.

"Marsh'l, can't you ask Mommy to stay here? I want to stay here."

"You do what your mother says. She knows what's right."

"I want to be where you are." Stevie watched him, fighting back the tears.

He looked from McQuade to his mother. She seemed to

115

be on the verge of speaking, but she remained silent. McQuade buttoned his coat, then squatted on his heels beside the boy. He knew how Stevie felt. When these things happened to someone so young it was extra hard. A few years older, it might be easier. He could only try to help a little.

"Maybe I'll come to Omaha and see you. You take care of your mother. You hear?"

Stevie had pressed close to McQuade, yet he wouldn't look at him. He stared at the floor, listening.

"I'll come to Omaha, I promise." McQuade squeezed the small shoulder and got to his feet. His throat was tight as he looked at Ann.

"I won't get down to the station," he said. "Once the railroad money's in, I can't leave the street."

Ann didn't move.

McQuade nodded to her, and at the boy. "Don't forget. I'm depending on you to take care of your mother."

He opened the door and went outside. Stevie sniffed and turned back to the hall. Ann stepped to the porch door. There were words in her mind she should have said. She wanted Dan to know she understood now why he had to stay. More than that, she wanted him to know she loved him, that she was leaving only for Stevie's good. But the words did not come, and McQuade disappeared into his office.

McQuade took the Greener shotgun from the rack and put a handful of shells into his pocket. He walked from the office to the center of Union. There was none of yesterday's early morning activity going on; the street was wide and deserted. He heard the approaching train's loudness, and was very much aware of the sun which beat down on him. Usually he hardly felt the heat, but in his weakened condition it seemed he sweated from every pore.

He was halfway to the station when he saw where the townsmen had gathered. They stood inside the livery doorway, their bodies shadowy outlines against the barn's dark interior. He gave them a casual glance, letting them know he was conscious of them before he mounted the platform steps.

Billy Ford stood near the ticket office. Beyond him was Stillwell and two armed men. The three stepped to the

116

edge of the platform when the train ground to a stop, black smoke pouring from its squat, barrel-like stack. Link-and-pin couplings clanged, break chains rattled and cars banged together as the slack came in.

The second the train was motionless the mail car door rolled back and three armed men carrying leather bags jumped down. Two others appeared from the engine and one more from the caboose. It all went so smoothly McQuade didn't move.

Stillwell and his two men fell in with the railroad guards. Half a minute later the nine of them were cutting past the storage shed behind the bank and up the alleyway.

Once they had turned into the bank's front porch, McQuade leaned against the rough boards of the depot. He felt into his pocket and took out the makings.

Billy grinned like a happy schoolboy. "That went off just as smooth," he said. "Won't be anyone tryin' t' get that money with all them guards."

McQuade gestured toward the bank. The six guards had reappeared from the porch and were returning to the train.

"You cover behind here," McQuade said. "I'll take the street."

Billy studied McQuade's side. "In the house," he said, "I didn't know you'd been hit bad."

McQuade nodded. "Anyone shows up out back, keep them here. Last thing we want is a gunfight with the street filled."

Billy headed for the rear of the bank, and McQuade left the platform. Now that he'd been on his feet this long, he realized the wisdom in Ann's words about his needing rest. He felt weak, as though his strength were slowly draining out of him.

Mayor Appell, standing inside the doorway of the blacksmith's, watched McQuade come slowly down Depot Street. Appell took no part in the low talk that was going on among the other men. Like them, he kept to the shadows so the marshal couldn't pick him out individually.

"I was damned mad when I heard 'bout all that money comin' in on the sly," the heavy-set blacksmith remarked. "But seein' how Stillwell's set things up, I go 'long with it.

Soon as Seth shows up, I'll get the wife and kids and take 'em to see that show."

"Sure," one of the younger men said, and he chuckled. "I wouldn't try holding back my kids. They'd make more trouble than any bank robbers could."

His chuckle, picked up by the rest, bloomed into laughter and relaxed talk, which lasted until the men began to leave for their places of business. Appell crossed the work area and moved along Union. He was passing the *Tribune* building when English opened the door and hailed him from the walk.

"Are you going to the bank this morning, John?" asked English.

"I am later. After I get the store opened."

"Tell Henry I'll come in, too, if he needs more guards for that money."

Appell stared at the newspaperman. "You're going to stay then? You'll keep Ann and the boy here?"

English shook his head. "They'll be leaving. I'll go in and help after I put them on the train. You tell Henry."

"All right," Appell answered. "I'll tell him."

Appell continued to his store, and English stepped back onto the *Tribune*'s porch. Quite a few people were out already, mostly children. English frowned as he watched them running around and playing on the platform. Then, when he saw Dingo Clinton appear beyond the depot, he opened the door, his frown deepening to a scowl.

He closed the door behind him and peered through the window. From beside the news press Jake Clinton said, "What's the matter?"

"Your cousin Dingo. He's riding in like he owns the town."

Dingo swung his horse to the left to cut along the side of the newspaper building. He wore no gun, nor was there a rifle in his saddle boot. Through the thin walls English could hear every clop of the animal's hoofs and the heavy thump of Dingo's boots as he dismounted. English didn't wait for him to knock. He pulled the door open.

Dingo stepped inside, carrying his bulky saddle roll over his shoulder. English closed the door, said, "What are you doing, coming in early like this?"

Dingo paid no attention to him. He looked directly at Jake. "I met a farmer on the road. That right 'bout Ed?"

Jake nodded, watching Dingo carefully. "He tried takin'

118

McQuade alone." One hand brushed over the dried blood on his pants leg. "I got this tryin' to help Ed."

Dingo didn't answer. He crossed the long room to lay the roll on the side table. Then he moved to the front windows and surveyed Union Street. "That the hotel with the big porch and saloon?"

"Yes," English told him. "Voci had the middle window."

Now Dingo nodded. "It'll be easy enough to get into." He returned to the table and began to unravel his saddle roll.

Jake Clinton said, "There's been a change, Dingo. I'm goin' t' be in that room."

Dingo's fingers let go of the roll. His eyes covered both men. "I'm goin' to be in there. That's how we said it. That's how it stays."

"No," Jake corrected. "You take the bank."

For thirty seconds Dingo simply looked at them. His right hand flipped open the roll, and they saw the short-barreled Winchester he had hidden inside. The hand dropped and rested dangerously on the carbine's stock while he spoke.

"You had your chance at McQuade. I get mine."

English said, "Hold it, now. We don't want to——"

"It's okay, English," Jake cut in. "Dingo can take McQuade." He nodded to his cousin. "As soon as we step out of the bank."

English remained quiet as Dingo lifted the rifle to check its load, his short stubby fingers deft and quick. Finally, he replaced the weapon and began to remake the roll.

Breathing easier, English opened the top desk drawer and took out his Remington derringer. He slid it into the top right pocket of his coat, then turned to Jake Clinton.

"Remember, Stillwell's the man you kill. Hit me just as hard as you hit the others. Just make certain it looks good."

Jake's head bobbed up and down slowly. His voice was sure, confident. "It'll look good," he said. "Damn good."

16

Dan McQuade sat alone in his office for almost an hour, until he heard the children begin shouting outside. Through the window he'd had a clear view of the front of the bank. Only one person, Mayor Appell, had gone inside during the morning. Now, at the yells, "The train! Here they come!" he saw Appell's face appear in the bank window.

McQuade stood. His side was stiff, but there was no tenderness or pain when he moved. He stopped at the edge of the walk. The sun beat down on him like a bellows blast, and he started to sweat.

The train was in plain view, its black smoke hovering over the prairie's western rim. Eight or ten boys had already broken into a run for the siding, to be close while the Wild West Show unloaded. Townspeople and farm families were lined along Union. Almost every child held a box of pop-corn or candied apple from the refreshment stand that had been set up on the restaurant porch.

Ann Heath saw all these things from George English's surrey as it came out of the alleyway into Union. She saw McQuade cross to the hotel and the cold blank stares he got from the people he passed.

Beside her, Stevie said, "Gee, Mommy, I wish we could stay."

Ann shook her head slowly, holding in a deep sigh. "It might come to Omaha," she said in a soft voice. "Remember?"

"I want to see it now, Mommy."

English turned the vehicle into Depot. Mentally, Ann considered the thought of remaining for the show. The temptation was there again, that sudden desire to give herself a chance to see how things would go. Then she shook her head quickly.

The team of matched bays slowed and stopped at the

station. English swung down to the platform, smiled and reached one arm up to help Ann.

"Mommy, can't we stay," Stevie begged. "Just till tonight."

"Oh, Stevie, don't keep after me."

"Mommy, please. I got to see it, Mommy. Please, Mommy."

Ann hesitated, her back pressed against the horsehair-stuffed seat. The train had reached the siding, and was backing in to unload the twelve brightly-painted cars that had *Carson's Prairie Exhibition* printed on their sides. Her eyes returned to English.

"I don't see why he has to miss it," she said. "We can leave our bags here till tonight."

"You can?" English's smooth face lost its smile. "Maybe I'm wrong. I'd thought you'd made up your mind. I thought you were sure."

She nodded her head, slowly.

"You should decide right now, Ann. We're not children. You know as well as I do there's more to this than just that show."

She glanced away to the line of spectators at the inter-section of Depot and Union. She could not push Dan out of her mind. Being with George didn't help, and she wasn't sure it would ever help. "I'm sorry if I seem foolish, George." Her soft smile asked for understanding. "I'm going to stay—for the show, anyway."

"Oh, boy!" Stevie yelped. "Boy, oh boy!" He started to climb over the opposite side of the surrey.

Ann took English's hand and stepped to the platform. She was near him, but she made no motion to go closer. For a second his arm was about her, and she felt him tremble. He moved back, breathing heavily.

"Just keep the boy clear of the bank," he said. "You can't tell— If there is trouble, I don't want you caught in it. I love you, Ann. You know that."

"We'll be with Mrs. Appell on the platform. We'll be safe."

English nodded, his face tight, serious. He spoke little while he walked Ann and the jubilant boy down Depot Street. Intense rage burned through him again, more hate-ful now than it had been last night. He held it in and calmed down a bit when he saw Dingo Clinton leave the

121

Tribune building and cross toward the hotel, his bulky saddle roll balanced casually on his shoulder.

The noise from Union grew louder. The Wild West Show had started to form up along the siding. A large open band-wagon was first in line, an ox-drawn prairie schooner behind it, then a stagecoach. Brightly-feathered Indians and Mexicans and cowboys waited on restless horses for the parade to begin.

English stayed close to Ann and Stevie until they were safely on the platform. He left them there and continued along the walk. From upper Farmington came the first sounds of the band, and children close by began yelling. English smiled at the people he passed, his eyes filled with the same interest and anticipation everyone else showed for the parade.

Millett was behind the hotel registration desk, busy counting the week's receipts when the screen door opened and Dingo Clinton came inside. The old clerk slid the money in a small canvas bag and put the bag into his side coat pocket as he watched the squat, black-bearded cowhand approach.

Dingo set his saddle roll on the desk, took off his sombrero and wiped his forehead with the back of his hand. "There's some rooms Major Carson reserv'd in here?" he said.

The clerk nodded. "Oh, yes. Two upstairs in the back." He paused, head cocked as he listened to the distant band music outside. "You ain't in the parade?"

"No. I'm gettin' things set up for the major. Didn't he say he was buyin' some cattle and saddles here?"

"Yes. Yes, he did. I guess you're all right." Millett turned and selected two keys from the rack. "Twenty-seven and -eight."

Dingo took the keys and lifted the roll.

"You'll have to sign in," Millett said. He opened the register on the counter.

Grunting, Dingo shouldered the roll and picked up the pen. "Major'll be wanting a bath," he said while he wrote. "You take care of that."

"Yes, certainly." Millett started into the kitchen.

He'd let the door close behind him and was halfway to the stove before he realized he'd not asked which room

Carson would use for the bath. He went back out to the lobby and crossed to the stairs.

The cowhand was on the second floor, but he'd stopped at Room 22. Outside in the street the drums were closer, and, as they boomed loudly, the cowhand lifted his booted foot and kicked the door open. He was in the room and had the door closed before Millett could yell.

Millett hurried up the stairs, angry at the way the cowhand had broken the door's lock. He'd been told the correct rooms and had no reason to bust the door in.

Millett opened the door without knocking. He saw the cowboy standing by the window turn fast, saw, without actually comprehending, the unraveled saddle roll on the bed and the stubby black-barreled rifle in the man's hands.

"This room's taken," Millett began. "The marshal—"

"Inside," snapped Dingo Clinton's low voice. "Shut the door easy." The barrel shifted inches to the heart.

Millett closed the door softly.

"Over to the side of the window," Dingo ordered. "Where I c'n keep an eye on you."

Millett edged close to the wall, paralyzed with fear.

Dingo reached out and jerked the canvas bag from the old clerk's pocket. He shook it open and looked inside. "Wal, damn me. If I didn't get a find here."

"That money's for the hotel. I just work for the owner," Millett pleaded. "I could never make up all that money."

"Shut up," Dingo ordered coldly. "Just shut up and stand there." He pulled the curtain aside an inch and stared out.

The bandwagon was opposite the school building. The cowhand musicians in ten-gallon hats and buckskin shirts made enough noise to drown out a gunshot. Directly behind rode Major Carson, a tall officer dressed in cavalry blue, leading a troop of straight-backed soldiers. A bonneted Indian chief and fifteen painted warriors sat bareback in a ragged line, followed by an equal number of Mexican vaqueros wearing bright serapes and huge sombreros.

Dingo's eyes surveyed the two lines of spectators. They stopped when they found McQuade walking toward the hotel porch. He nodded and smiled. McQuade was close enough to get with a hand gun, and would be a sure kill with the carbine.

Dingo eyed the old clerk and made certain he couldn't interfere. Then he drew the cane-backed chair close to the window and sat down to wait.

English had paused to watch until the cowboys driving twenty long-horned steers at the end of the parade turned the cattle ito Depot Street. He glanced over the hotel porch again and saw Dingo's shadow behind the middle window.

Major Carson was galloping his gray charger back along the line of the parade. Abreast of the grandstand, he pulled up the horse onto its hind legs, forefeet in the air. The animal bowed on one knee, while Carson gave a snappy military salute to a storm of children's yells and applause.

From upper Union a bugle sounded. The audience quieted.

"Ladies and gentlemen," Carson announced, "permit me to introduce the equestrian portion of the Wild West Exhibition." He looked around at his performers. "Carson's Wild West, are you ready?"

The band blared. Tom-toms boomed. Indians shrieked, and cowboys and Mexicans answered with whooping yells.

English moved on again. But he halted the moment he spotted Gruber on the hardware porch.

English muttered under his breath and walked quickly to where Gruber stood. "What are you waiting for," he asked angrily.

Gruber stared at him. "I didn't see anybody move any cattle in so they can drive 'em into the street. I wasn't sure—"

"We're not using the cattle. Yates has already blown the tracks twenty miles south of here, you fool. They'll be going into the bank in ten minutes."

A sudden outbreak of children's shouting made Gruber glance at the street. Three riders, a Mexican, an Indian and a cowboy, raced around the bend at upper Union, the Mexican in the lead. Gruber's eyes returned to English. "Look, Mr. English. There are too many kids out there."

"Get over to McQuade."

"But there are so many kids."

"What do you want? For Clinton to come after you?"

Gruber gulped. The yelling spectators had quieted. He heard Carson's voice call out, "Next on our program, an

124

exhibition of daredevil riding coupled with superb marksmanship. Look toward the west end of the street, ladies and gentlemen!"

"I need a drink, Mr. English," Gruber said. "Let me get a drink?"

"Get one. Make it look like you're drunk. Anything you want. But you be sure McQuade's busy with you when we move."

Gruber looked toward the hotel porch where McQuade had stopped. He bit down on his lower lip nervously. "He will be, Mr. English. He will be."

17

A RANGY COWBOY RODE AT breakneck speed down the center of Union Street, the six-guns he held shattering glass balls Major Carson threw high into the air over the heads of the crowd. Opposite the platform the cowboy reined in hard. He leaped to the ground, seized his Spencer rifle from its boot and blasted three more balls before they started to fall.

"And there you have Mr. Art Clover," Major Carson called. "The Cowboy Kid!"

The marksman bowed and led his horse toward Depot while the street resounded with cheers and applause.

"Keep your eyes on the Indians," announced Major Carson. "A portion of the Pawnee Tribe will demonstrate their native pastimes. They will first present a Pawnee Tribal war dance!"

Tom-toms thumped as ten half-naked, painted warriors stepped into Union from the sideline. They started to form a ragged circle, dancing slowly to the beat of the drums.

Dan McQuade, crossing the hotel porch, had moved to the top step to watch, but now his attention centered on the man who was knocking on the bank door. It was George English. Appell was the one who opened the door to let the newspaperman inside.

McQuade shook his head. The fools realized there was no danger to the bank as long as that door stayed shut. There they were, opening it, inviting trouble. McQuade remained at the edge of the porch, his eyes intent on the bank. Across the street Billy Ford came out of the alley alongside the jail.

Billy pushed through the crowd directly for the porch. Frowning, McQuade started down the steps.

The deputy began talking as soon as he met McQuade. "Seth Perrault's been killed," he said. "The Ortegas found him in the river. He's over behind the jail."

McQuade nodded and glanced back toward the audience, his eyes stopping where Ann stood with Steven on the platform. She had looked away from the Indians, and was watching their talk.

"Hey, Ann didn't—" Billy began.

"She's been there since the train left," McQuade said. He started across Union. "Watch the bank until I get back."

McQuade hurried down the alleyway to the rear of the jail. A Mexican couple were waiting beside their small farm wagon near the barn. The man was old and short-legged, as dark as an Indian. He moved ahead of McQuade to the tailboard. He pointed to the hand of a man that was protruding from beneath the lumped canvas inside the wagon.

"We find him in the river, Marsh'l," he said. "Four miles out of town, on a sand bar."

Nodding, McQuade raised the canvas. Beside him the Mexican woman crossed herself and mumbled a prayer. McQuade stared at the dead man, his face grim and harsh.

There was nothing but a mass of pulpy black and white and red instead of Seth Perrault's face. He'd been beaten unmercifully, possibly in an attempt to make him unrecognizable. And he had been found four miles away, so whoever had done this hadn't figured on the body being washed up on a sand bar. The rustle of a dress behind him made him look around.

Ann had come into the yard. "Billy told me they'd found Seth. Oh, Dan—" Her face was pale, twisted.

"Where's Steve?"

"He's all right. I left him with Mrs. Appell when I saw you come back here." She shook her head slowly. "Who'd do a thing like that?"

"Ruthless, merciless men," he said as he lowered the canvas. "When they think the law can't get them. If they figure it isn't strong enough."

She didn't answer. Her eyes remained on the wagon, and she rubbed her forehead with the tips of her fingers. McQuade said to the Mexican, "Leave the wagon in the barn. Don't tell anyone about this."

"*Si,*" the man said respectfully. "We can stay here?"

"Just do as you'd planned. I'll see you after the show."

127

He left them and walked back to the street, keeping his stride slow enough for Ann to stay abreast of him.

Billy said on the walk, "No one's gone inside the bank."

"Better get back there," McQuade said. "Remember, don't try to handle anything alone."

His eyes followed the deputy as he moved along the street. Then McQuade stepped into his office. He lifted a Winchester .73 from the rack and checked its load. Outside the audience was silent as they watched the Pawnees dance. The Indians' yells and shrieks had become louder and wilder with the increased tempo of the thumping drums. McQuade tucked the carbine under his left arm and went back onto the walk.

Ann fell in beside McQuade when he recrossed Union. None of the spectators turned to look at them. Everybody was watching the Pawnees, fascinated by the violence of the war dance. McQuade did not stop until he was on the porch of the building opposite the bank.

"Better keep clear of me," he said quietly to Ann.

Ann stared at him, her face grave. "You don't have to make yourself a target like this."

He scanned the opposite building. His eyes rested on the bank window for a few seconds, then returned to her. A wisp of fine blonde hair hung down over her forehead and stirred in the slight wind. "I don't have a choice," he said. "You go ahead. I'll find you afterward."

"Afterward?" she repeated slowly.

He smiled into her worried face and put a hand on her arm. For just that instant they stood together in silence, oblivious of the shouting and cheering that broke out as the Indian dance ended. "I'll find you," he said again, quietly.

His eyes followed her until she was within the crowd. He rolled a cigarette and stood in the hot sunlight, smoking as though he were watching only the show. He was aware of the empty bank porch, the long alleyway on both sides of the building. He also saw Gruber come out of the hotel saloon, staggering a bit. McQuade paid little attention to the big, flabby man.

Then he noticed that Gruber was coming along the walk, directly toward where he stood.

Billy Ford glanced around at McQuade before he

128

turned in at the rear of the bank. He noted how McQuade was waiting, letting himself be seen by anyone who went up on the bank porch, offering himself as a target instead of the people who were watching the show. Billy thought of that, and then of the marshal's weakness in the house that morning. He understood McQuade's hardness now, and the strength of the man.

All thoughts of McQuade died the instant Billy rounded the corner and saw the men, three of them, leading horses behind the storage shed. The three stopped short, guns in their hands, before Billy could make a motion to draw. The biggest one Billy recognized as Frenchy, and he remembered Jessup from the card game.

Jake Clinton stepped forward. "Hold it there. Right there."

Billy tried to say something, but he couldn't speak or move.

Clinton came closer, his eyes on Billy's gun hand. "Just like that. Quiet-like."

Then he was beside Billy, jerking the deputy's Colt from its holster. He opened the revolver and dropped the bullets to the ground. He snapped it closed and shoved it back into the holster.

"Get a good look, Jessup," he ordered. "See if it's clear."

Jessup stepped to the corner and peered carefully up the alleyway.

Billy told them, "You haven't got a chance. That street's covered from both ends."

"Gruber's goin' up to McQuade now," Jessup said over his shoulder. "We gotta move fast."

"Okay, walk." Jake Clinton motioned with his six-gun. "Up to the porch."

Billy looked at him, not moving.

Frenchy shoved the deputy from behind and forced him to take a step forward. "Go 'head," he snarled. "Ask for a broken head."

Clinton gave Billy another rough shove, jabbing the barrel into the small of his back. "You don't try goin' slow. One move, I'll kill you. You think of that."

"Keep your eyes on the burros!" Major Carson called. "I have the honor of introducing Mustang Pete, or, as the

129

Indians named him, 'Pet-se-ka-we-cha-cha,' the great high jumper!"

"McQuade!" Gruber's loud voice called, taking McQuade's attention away from the cowboys who were lining two burros in the street, while at the far end of Union a rider was waiting on a tall white horse to begin the high-jump exhibition. "McQuade, the gun-happy lawboy! You still here?"

McQuade glanced to the left and checked Gruber's stance. Those in the crowd close to the porch had turned to stare.

"Thought they'd told you to git last night, McQuade!"

"You're drunk, Gruber," said McQuade calmly. "Don't make any mistakes."

Gruber took a step nearer. He glowered drunkenly and flexed his thick arms like a boxer waiting to come out of his corner. McQuade watched him and the faces near them. They'd lost their surprised expressions, and were waiting with anticipation.

"You're gonna git, McQuade. Git walkin'. Or do I make you?"

McQuade shook his head. "You get walking, Gruber. I'll knock you down where you stand."

A man shouted, "Go 'head, Grub! Get 'im!"

"Yeah—yeah! Get him, Gruber!"

Gruber flexed his arms again and then heisated. Someone chuckled. Others broke into laughter and talk that was drowned out by the pounding of horse's hoofs, then the spontaneous thundering of applause as the white horse cleared the burros. Gruber's eyes flicked to the crowd.

McQuade turned his head to look across the street, letting the people know he had only the bank on his mind. Gruber grabbed at the opportunity. He charged in and smashed out with a vicious, slashing punch. The men circled around and started yelling.

McQuade, whirling in a complete turn, took the blow on his left shoulder. Pain shot through his wounded side, and he staggered back on the porch, pulling his Colt as he regained balance.

Gruber's big body pressed close, both arms extended to seize McQuade and throw him to the floor.

White-hot agony filled McQuade's chest. He tried to side-step, feeling blood ooze along his side. His right arm swung wide, brought the steel barrel squarely down on Gruber's head.

Gruber grunted and fell forward, his outstretched hands grabbing McQuade's arm and dragging McQuade down with him.

18

Inside the bank Mayor Appell's face was pressed to the door window. "Gruber's got McQuade down," he told the others. "I'll be darned if he hasn't. No, no, McQuade's getting up."

English stepped to the door with Stillwell. He couldn't see McQuade clearly because of the men who'd crowded around. He did know that Appell had left his Starr revolver on the counter of the closest teller's cage. Thompson, Stillwell's teller, had been making a cigarette when Appell noticed the fight. He was still holding the tobacco and paper as he looked through the long window, so he'd have trouble reaching for the .45 holstered at his side.

"That fool Gruber," Stillwell said angrily. "He'll spoil everything we've planned."

"I'll go over there and see what I can do," English offered.

"No," Stillwell answered. "That's the mayor's job. You get over there, Appell." He turned the key in the lock and began to pull open the door. "You straighten out McQuade, too. Let him know—"

His words ceased as the door swung back in his face. Jake Clinton stepped inside first, Colt cocked and ready to fire, his other hand shoving Appell away from the doorway. Jessup and Frenchy were a step behind Billy Ford, whom Frenchy was pushing inside. Jessup shut the door and yanked down the shades. He inched the window shade aside and looked out.

"We're clear," he said. "McQuade's still busy with Gruber."

Clinton pointed to the safe. "Get everything out, banker. Fast about it."

"Wha—what?" Stillwell stuttered, dumfounded at the suddenness of what had happened.

"Everything in the safe. Damn fast." Clinton grabbed the banker's shoulder and dragged him toward the safe.

Thompson dropped the tobacco and papers as Clinton went past, and the teller's hand fell to his side. Clinton swung out and chopped down with the steel barrel. It caught the teller solidly above the ear, and Thompson groaned, knees buckling. He toppled and hit the floor with a loud thud.

English said, "You won't get away with this."

"Shut up!" Frenchy's huge fist gripped the newspaperman's coat front and swung him against the wall. "Keep shut. All of you."

At the safe, Clinton said, "Open it." A smile came over his face, making a subtle change in his eyes, around his mouth.

Mechanically, Stillwell started to unlock the safe.

Appell shuffled his feet nervously. He looked at the Starr .44 he'd left on the counter.

"One move," Frenchy said. "One move, you."

"Don't try it," Billy warned Appell. "He'll shoot."

"Damned right I'll shoot. Just try me."

Clinton glanced around at Jessup. "How is it?"

"McQuade's got Gruber. He's clearin' a way from the porch. Takin' him to the jail."

Clinton's eyes returned to Stillwell. The gun in his hand moved closer to the banker's head. "Hurry up."

Stillwell fumbled with the safe's lock, then pulled open the heavy iron door. Clinton shoved him aside and, bending over, reached in and took the first leather bag. He handed this and the second one to Frenchy. The last two he kept himself.

"Okay, close it," he told Stillwell.

The banker pushed the door shut, and his face filled with sudden fear the instant Clinton raised the barrel of the Colt. He had no time to pull away before the weapon struck the side of his head. He crumpled to the pine floor like an empty sack.

Appell had a fraction of a second, long enough to take a step back in the realization he was going to be hurt. Frenchy wasted no time. His huge fist swung wide and clipped the nape of the mayor's neck, knocking him senseless.

"Okay, you two," Clinton said, eyeing Billy and English. He crossed to the newspaperman, reached into his coat

133

pocket and came out with the derringer. Clinton threw the weapon behind the safe and stared into English's surprised face. "We walk out fast and 'round to the shed. One trick, we start shootin'."

English said in a low voice, "What are you trying?"

Jake Clinton grinned widely. "You'll see quick enough." He pushed English toward the door. Frenchy slammed Billy's back. "Get movin'."

Jessup dropped the shade. "Wait up. McQuade's crossin' the street. Give him time to reach the jail."

Suddenly Jake Clinton laughed. "Easy," he said. "All the plannin'. And it was damned easy."

McQuade studied the crowd. He hadn't wanted to take the time to lock up Gruber, but he had no other choice. The fight had excited the spectators, and his arresting Gruber had angered most of them. Those near him paid no attention to the high-jump exhibition. They had moved in close to him, forming a solid line that bellied out from the walk clear across Union.

He didn't believe trouble would come, but he couldn't be sure. His not being sure of the bank caused him to glance that way. He halted, transfixed for a moment, comprehending what the drawn shades meant.

Gruber understood, too. He stepped closer to McQuade. "Let it go, Marshal. Let it go."

"Get going." He jerked the Winchester at the jail. "We reach the walk, start running down the alley."

"Kids, Marshal. Too many kids!"

"Move."

Gruber shook his head wildly and extended both hands to grab the rifle barrel. Sharp pain cut deep into McQuade's side. He let go of the Winchester and drew his Colt as Gruber wrenched up the stock. Gruber danced to the left, putting his big body between McQuade and the hotel while he brought the barrel around.

"Don't try it," McQuade snapped. "Don't."

A rifle cracked from the hotel window. Gruber's mouth opened in shock as the steel slug smashed the middle of his broad back, breaking his spine. Fearful screams rose from the crowd. Those in the rear panicked and began to run, the ones in the front scattering fanwise.

McQuade's surprise lasted just long enough for him to aim at the hotel window. The rifle slammed once more in

134

the instant McQuade got his shot off. He was moving when the bullet sliced the heel of his shoe.

He heard his slug crash through the window. He slowed, looking around for a path clear of the terrified mob. Only the street beyond the jail was open. The corner of his eye caught the bank door swinging in and men coming out. People between him and the bank ran wildly, their screams and yells unintelligible.

McQuade saw the shadow of a man behind the shattered hotel window and the rifle barrel, which pushed the curtain aside again and aimed at him.

McQuade triggered three shots at the window, but the shadowy figure pulled back before the bullets smashed the glass.

McQuade was moving past the jail, away from the hotel. His left hand plucked cartridges from his belt and held them until he could slow to reload.

A man's voice shouted, "He's running! Lookit that! He's runnin'!"

"Dan? Dan?" McQuade heard a woman call from behind him. He knew it was Ann, but he couldn't turn.

Clear of the crowd now, he kept running.

Dingo Clinton had jerked his stubby body away from the window for the second it took McQuade's bullets to smash into the room. He peeked out now, Winchester aimed.

McQuade was gone. Gruber's motionless body was alone in the street, except for a woman who'd run out toward him. The thought that McQuade was inside the hotel flashed through Dingo's mind, but it vanished as quickly when he saw that the people who were cowering in the alleyways were all looking toward the jail.

McQuade was crossing the walk there, to go into the alley. Dingo left the window and started out of the room. He'd faced men like McQuade before, and knew the lawman had run only to take the fight away from the people.

"My money. Give me my money," Millett begged. He'd stepped from the wall, and was going toward the door.

Dingo hesitated, waiting until Millett came closer. He jabbed out the wooden stock and hit the old clerk below the jawbone. Millett staggered back into the corner.

Dingo pulled open the door and went into the hallway.

135

Millett struggled to his feet. Too dizzy to stand alone, he had to lean against the wall, then hold on to the doorknob to keep his balance. He stared dazedly at the stairs, hearing Dingo's boots clomp loudly through the lobby. His muddled brain cleared, then filled with thoughts of his money, his job.

He began to walk, gasping for breath, rubbing at the soreness along his jaw and neck. He felt stronger by the time he reached the registration desk. The Greener shotgun was exactly where he'd put it. Millett broke into a run once he had it in his hands.

On the porch, he stopped.

Dingo was out of range across Union, going along the walk very carefully. Two blocks ahead of him was the woman who'd run out to Gruber's dead body. Carrying the rifle McQuade had left in the street, she had stopped to stare down the alleyway between the milliner's and the restaurant. She paused only a fraction of a minute before she moved on to the restaurant block.

Dingo, staying close to the front of the buildings, followed along behind her. She'd lead the gunman to McQuade, Millett knew. McQuade, who had been right all along, who'd stuck to the town even when it didn't deserve it . . .

Millett went slowly down to the street. The hot, driving sun brought back his dizziness, and he staggered. He gripped the shotgun tighter and tried to keep from stumbling as he walked.

19

M CQUADE WAS MOVING ALONG THE rear of the restaurant when the gunmen emerged from beside the bank. Jake Clinton was in the lead, followed by English and Jessup. Last was Frenchy, who shoved Billy ahead of him, forcing the deputy to keep up. Jake saw McQuade, halted where he stood and triggered a shot while he yelled for the others to get back to cover.

McQuade pushed himself away from the building. The high whine of the slug tore past him and whacked loudly into the clapboards. As he started to run for the corner of the hardware store, he got off a shot, putting the bullet high so not to hit Billy or English.

Sliding in next to the hardware store, he could hear confused, quick talk going on among the gunmen.

McQuade fired again to keep them behind cover, and then silence fell. McQuade called, "You can't get to those horses. Throw out your guns."

Silence again.

McQuade's tall body trembled all over, and he pressed against the building. The hot throbbing in his side, which had become worse during his run, wouldn't calm down. He pressed his body closer and waited.

Guns blasted from the bank, the zinging bullets clearly intended to make him keep his cover. McQuade heard the loud thump of boots running on sand, and he stepped across to the side of the restaurant. Frenchy, head down and body crouched, was making a dash for the horses behind the storage shed. McQuade aimed his Colt and squeezed the trigger.

The bullet hit Frenchy in the chest. The huge man slowed and staggered, but he continued his run.

McQuade aimed once more, but he didn't fire, because Frenchy's big body began to go down after five long

137

strides. He hit the ground hard, went sliding through the dust a few feet, then lay still.

"Throw out those guns," McQuade yelled.

Suddenly, at a sound behind him, he turned and swung the muzzle of the Colt.

"No, Dan! No!" Ann Heath came down the alleyway, holding his Winchester out to him.

"Stay back, Ann!"

She didn't stop but moved in beside him, holding her body close to the building. "You won't have a chance without this." She was breathing deeply, panting for air.

He took the carbine. "Get back now."

"Your side. It's bleeding again."

"Forget my side. They've got Billy and English with them."

"They can't go anywhere," she said, looking at the horses. She was still panting, but her breath was coming easier now. "All you have to do is hold them till help comes."

"They might charge. Get clear, Ann."

Ann edged away toward the head of the alleyway, and McQuade turned and gave his attention to the clearing between the gunmen and the storage shed.

In the heavy silence he could hear bits of talk near the bank. He waited for some sound of movement, some hint that Jake Clinton and Jessup might try a break for the horses. The only sound came from behind him, a loud gasp from Ann.

"Dan!"

McQuade whirled and saw Dingo Clinton standing at the street entrance to the alleyway, a stub-barreled carbine in his hands.

McQuade straightened and moved into the center of the alley to make Dingo shift his fire away from Ann. Dingo took two steps closer and aimed the rifle, not giving McQuade a chance to bring his Winchester up.

Dingo never fired. The deafening blast of a shotgun exploded in the street behind Dingo, tearing the gunman's back apart. He was blown forward like a tree felled by a vicious wind.

Millett appeared a second later, the Greener he was holding still smoking in his hand. He bent over the dead gunman and began going through his pockets.

Ann ran toward McQuade. He stood with one shoulder

against the restaurant wall, his left hand holding his side, deep lines of pain cut into his face.

"I told you to get back," he said tightly.

"No. You're hurt."

"Go ahead."

"No. Dan, I understand now. You needed that rifle, but you left it so the people—"

"I'm letting them make their break. I can't with you here."

He glanced into the clearing, then gazed angrily at her, staring into a face as determined as his own. She pressed closer to him and let some of his weight rest on her, so near he felt how her body shook. All the time he'd waited, all his patience, had been worth this. He wanted to reach out and hold her to him, but he drove the impulse from his mind.

"Do what I say," he said. "You get back now."

Her face calmed, and she nodded her head. "When they start, I will, Dan. When they start."

Jake Clinton crouched like a runner on his mark. "You let him have the whole load," he told Jessup. "We'll make the horses."

"When you're ready," Jessup said, "let me know."

Clinton slid his body along to the corner of the bank. He glanced at Billy, then at English. "Lie flat, you two."

"You won't get far," English warned, hate filling his face. "Not after this robbery."

"Down," Clinton ordered. "Figure you're lucky to get out of it alive."

English dropped to his knees and stretched out. But Billy took his time.

"Damn you goin' so slow," Clinton growled. "We'd been outta here now if you'd moved faster." He swung his revolver around threateningly toward the deputy.

"No, Jake," warned Jessup. "If we don't make it, we ain't killed nobody."

"Cut that," Clinton snapped. "We'll damn well make it."

Billy lay motionless, his head flat against the dirt, his eyes staring into Clinton's. The gunman tightened his fingers on the moneybags and jerked up the barrel of his gun. "Okay. Okay, let's go, Jess."

Jessup opened fire. He started out behind Clinton when

the first of his six bullets whanged into the opposite alleyway. Clinton reached the safety of the shed before Jessup's last shot sounded. Jessup, still ten feet from the small building, suddenly realized he'd used up all his bullets. He quickened his stride, a wild, uncontrollable panic gripping him. He watched Clinton, waiting for him to turn and give him cover fire.

"Jake! Jake!"

McQuade's rifle cracked. Jessup grabbed his right shoulder and went down. Beyond him, Clinton had untied the black stallion and was climbing into the saddle. Jessup crawled toward him, both his hands clawing madly at the earth.

"Jake! Pick me up, Jake!"

Clinton swung the horse and headed for the flat across the railroad tracks.

Billy Ford pushed himself to his feet and dashed to where Frenchy lay. He reached the dead gunman as McQuade's carbine thundered twice. Clinton, just pulling out from behind the storage shed, swung his mount to the left. He straightened the animal before it had turned fully around, to make his escape with the shed between himself and McQuade.

"Get him," McQuade yelled to Billy. "Get him."

Billy had both of Frenchy's six-guns. One he threw back to English. "Hold him," he called, pointing to Jessup. And he ran for the shed.

Jessup, on his knees, threw his good arm over his head. "No! No, you take me!" he screamed. He made a terrified grab to hold back Billy, but, failing, he stared frantically into the weapon in English's hand.

As Billy reached the shed, he realized what his only chance to stop Clinton was. He aimed the Colt, fired low, once, again and again.

The bullets struck the stallion's flank, thudding in like the muffled cracks of a whip. The horse, whinnying in panic, slowed. Clinton fought to hold it steady, but the animal pulled to the right and turned in a half circle back toward the shed. It hadn't completed the turn fully when it began to stumble.

Clinton went down with his mount, was thrown forward and sent skidding along the dusty ground.

Billy was on top of him before he rolled to a stop.

Clinton tried to jump up, the Colt in his hand cocked

and pointed at Billy. The deputy's left arm swung out and knocked the weapon aside. It exploded, the bullet plowing harmlessly into the ground. Billy brought his gun barrel down savagely into the gunman's face.

Clinton, crying out in pain, attempted to fall away and clear. Billy followed him down, caught in the violence of his fight. He didn't plan or think; he just acted, all the pent-up fear and lack of confidence that had made him a failure as a lawman unleashed in his attack.

He straightened at the sight of Clinton sprawled flat, the gunman's body twisted awkwardly, neither hand reaching for the fallen revolver. Billy jerked the Colt at Clinton's head.

"Up fast," Billy ordered. He wiped his forehead with his shirt sleeve and drew a deep breath.

Jake Clinton moaned, holding both hands to his head. His eyes were clouded, glazed with pain and hate. They switched to his six-gun in the dust.

"Try it, I'll kill you," Billy said calmly.

Clinton's eyes, clearing, showed sudden fear. He pushed himself onto his knees quickly and stood.

Billy, stepping aside to let his prisoner pass, glanced at the alleyway and saw that McQuade had come out. He also saw that Jessup was on his feet, making an effort to back away from the revolver in English's hand.

"Go ahead," he heard English say in a low voice. "Start running. I'll shoot you where you stand."

McQuade didn't hear English's words, but he did see Jessup's uncontrolled fear and heard him plead, "Don't let him shoot! He's behind this whole thing! He—"

"Shut up, you gunman," English spat. "You killers come into a decent town and threaten everyone. You both deserve to die."

"He's in this!" Jessup called to McQuade. "He planned it so's Voci'd be in that hotel room to cut you down. You come in early and forced the whole thing." He turned to Clinton and added, "Tell him, Jake! You tell him?"

Clinton stared worriedly at English, then at the weapon in the newspaperman's hand. "No, he wasn't in on nothin'." His eyes switched to Jessup, but his voice was for English. "Just be damned careful what you do."

"It was English's idea, I tell you!" Jessup screamed.

"Listen, he got Gruber fired so's he'd help. He even took care of that hostler. He shut him up."

McQuade spoke quickly, watching both Jessup and English. "What about the hostler?"

"He's dead. English—" Jessup shied away from the threatening Colt and stepped fearfully toward McQuade. "Ask Jake. He was there."

"What are you trying?" English snapped. "I'm not going to let you pull anything like this."

"Let him talk," McQuade said.

"What? You'll listen to a gunman?"

"I'll listen to what he has to say about Seth."

"Jake told me English killed the hostler. Get Jake inside. He'll talk. Look—English fixed it up for Appell to hire you. There was someone here he was sure you'd come to see. He said you'd take the marshal's job just so you could be here. He did, Marsh'l! He did!"

McQuade nodded and said to English, "I'll take that gun. He was aware of Ann watching, standing beside him stiffly, her face fearful. "You'll have your say, English."

English shook his head and shifted the Colt's barrel to McQuade. A townsman had appeared at the mouth of the bank alleyway, then two more men, Appell and Stillwell, who stopped a few feet beyond the buildings and kept quiet to hear what was going on.

"I'm walking out of here," English said tightly. "I'm not letting these gunmen tie me in with them."

"I want to know how they learned about Seth Perrault," McQuade said. "Drop the gun."

"I'm not dropping anything. Not until I'm allowed to walk out of here."

"You'll get a shot off, maybe," said McQuade in a sure voice. "Before I go down, I'll get you, mister."

English, eyeing McQuade's Winchester, brought the Colt's barrel up, directly into McQuade's face.

McQuade didn't move, thinking how ridiculous this was, facing English in such a sure thing for them both. After all the bad, dangerous men he'd faced, knowing each time it could be the last for him—in a saloon, walking the middle of a hot, dusty street, a bushwhack, but not like this . . .

Billy Ford's words came calmly. "I hear a click, English, you're a dead man."

McQuade said, "One second now."

English's body stiffened. He bit his lips, studying the two lawmen uncertainly. He gazed at Ann and shook his head hopelessly. The Colt dropped from his fingers.

McQuade wiped the sweat from his forehead, his hand trembling. "Lock them up," he said to Billy.

The deputy stared at him and gave him a confident smile. "Right, Marshal."

McQuade nodded. His eyes moved to the elderly hotel clerk, who was standing with the shotgun in one hand, his canvas moneybag in the other. "Thanks, Mr. Millett," he said quietly. Then he turned and looked at Ann.

The townspeople crowding the alleyway didn't move as Billy led the three prisoners away. Stillwell, one hand holding a handkerchief against his bruised head, stood motionless beside Appell. Like the rest, they were stunned by what had happened. McQuade didn't blame them. He could read the same stunned expression on Ann's face.

But her eyes shifted from English's back to McQuade's wounded side. "I'll go to the doctor's with you, Dan."

She fell silent as she saw the way McQuade was surveying the crowd. Mrs. Appell, a short, gray-haired woman, had pushed her way through to the mayor. With her was Stevie, the boy's small face tight, worried. When he saw his mother he grinned happily, then ran toward her.

"Dan," Ann went on softly, "that talk about Arizona. If you decide to go ... " She became silent, studied his face.

McQuade looked at Stevie, who had almost reached them. He gazed at the grouped faces, the mixture of men and women and children, townspeople, farmers, some of the Wild West crew. A murmur had started among them, and a few of the more curious drifted toward Frenchy's body. The talk, the sound of the crowd, was different somehow. McQuade waited, puzzled.

Then, suddenly, he realized the fear and hostility were gone. There was no trace of hate. "Tombstone might make you remember," he said, meeting Ann's stare. "You'd still go?"

"Wherever you go, Dan."

Stevie reached his mother, his wide eyes excited. "You got them, Marsh'l. Them bad men could've shot you."

"They didn't," McQuade told him. "Come along with your mother, Steve."

The boy took his mother's hand, and they began to

walk with McQuade. Behind them the talk grew louder. Stillwell's voice sounded above the others. "Marshal? You're not leaving, Marshal?"

McQuade turned. His glance ran across the watching faces. "There could be other Clintons," he said. "Or other gunmen."

"We know," Appell said. "We'll worry about that if it comes."

Stillwell added, "That's right, Marshal. They won't try facing this whole town." Those close to the banker picked up his words and echoed them.

McQuade nodded.

"You'll stay then, Marshal?" asked Stillwell.

Dan McQuade looked beyond the crowd. Union was deserted back there. The bandwagon and stagecoach stood alone in the middle of the dusty street. McQuade gestured toward them.

"You've got a show to finish. I'll be out later with my deputy."

He felt Ann's hand tighten on his arm, and he saw Stevie's happy face. He heard the talk start up again. Someone laughed nervously. Then more laughter—safe, contented laughter.

They continued walking.

McQuade studied the big barn two blocks ahead of him. He was remembering the shingles that needed to be replaced on the roof, the cleaning that had to be done inside. He thought of the house beyond, and the safety and peace he had found there last night. He looked at the woman holding the hand of the child beside her—the woman who would be in that house with him.